Fraser, Anthea

The Stone

THE STONE

Those with long memories in the Chiltern village of Ickfield treat their megalith with increasing respect as its sinister cycle comes round again, but the Prior family, engaged in moving into their new home on the hillside directly beneath it, know nothing of the Stone's dark history.

Unfortunately, their ignorance affords them no protection against the pagan forces which have dramatically disrupted the lives of others who lived in that house before them. A hundred-year-old diary and some curious pebbles alert local antique dealer Adam Sandys to possible danger, but despite his vigilance and that of her elder sister Hilary, fifteen-year-old Vanessa becomes increasingly disturbed by the malign influence of the Stone until subconsciously she comes to accept that it is she who is responsible for providing it with yet another human sacrifice.

THE STONE

Anthea Fraser

ST. MARTIN'S PRESS
NEW YORK

ROBERT HALE LIMITED
LONDON

Photoset by
Specialised Offset Services Limited, Liverpool
and printed in Great Britain by
Clarke, Doble & Brendon Limited
Plymouth, Devon

One

Up on the hillside above Ickfield the long grasses which
brushed against the rough surface of the Druid Stone
shivered at the contact. The hill-top rabbits had long
ceased to play around its base and a pheasant, momentarily
alighting on it took off again with a clatter of nervous wings.
For the emanations were becoming stronger and those
creatures dependent on instinct for their survival
recognized and feared them.

The Prior family, however, their instincts blunted by
centuries of civilization, were that day preparing to move
into the house immediately below.

"Not much farther now," Julia said rallyingly to her son
and daughter in the back seat of the car.

"Let's hope the vans arrive on time," Gavin remarked.
"Anything can happen during two hundred miles and an
overnight stop."

"Well, we'll soon know." She settled back contentedly
and looked out of the window. "It'll be just like old times,
being back in Buckinghamshire and able to have a day in
London again, with –"

She broke off abruptly and after a moment's silence
Gavin said quietly, "You were going to say 'with Marion',
weren't you?"

"I just – wasn't thinking. I suppose the point is that I've
never really accepted it, and being so far away it was easy to
pretend to myself that it hadn't happened. Not any more,
though. I'm dreading having to go and see her."

"Brian said she's been counting the days till we arrive."

"I know."

Her husband glanced at her and adroitly changed the subject. "Did you tell the men ten o'clock?"

"It was they who told me! But if by any miracle they arrive before we do, Mrs Hare will be able to let them in. The Dentons left the key with her and she was going to clean everywhere while it was empty."

"I'm not sure I care for the thought of an unknown woman letting us into our own house! Wasn't it a bit rash taking her on like that, sight unseen?"

"Not at all. Even if she hadn't been asking such a ridiculously low wage I'd have jumped at the chance of keeping her. She's been with the Dentons since they moved in last September and they spoke very highly of her. It's all right for you, leaving the house at eight-thirty every morning, but if I'm not to be tied to it permanently I'll need some help."

"Did the people before us only come last September?" Vanessa asked suddenly from the back seat.

"Apparently, yes."

"It's hard luck having to move again so soon," Nick commented.

"Actually they didn't have to. Mr Denton's still working in High Wycombe, I believe. Perhaps they found it was too big for just the two of them. Anyway, I'm very glad they did decide to go, and that Brian told us about the house the minute it came on the market. You'll love it, darlings, I know you will."

It was going to be another hot day. Even at this early hour windows were flung open to catch a breath of air and as they turned into Ickfield High Street the shopkeepers were rolling out their sun-blinds. Moments later Gavin turned left, skirting the village green and duckpond and following the small road which circled round behind them. There was no sign of the removal vans, but their first sight of Conningley showed that at least the inestimable Mrs

Hare had arrived, for the front door stood invitingly open. Gavin drew up to one side of it, leaving plenty of room for the vans.

"There's not much point in unloading the car at this stage," he remarked, "since we've nowhere to put anything until the furniture arrives. You two can go and have a quick look round if you like, but come back as soon as you hear the vans."

Vanessa climbed slowly out of the car and stood stretching, looking up at the house with its graceful Georgian windows and the wistaria growing round the door. The morning sun was on her face, yet for some reason a little shiver trickled over her. Without waiting for her brother to come round the car she set off towards the open door. She had a brief impression of sun-filled space, of bare shining boards, and then, as she stepped over the threshold, total blackness.

It was Nick's shout of alarm that alerted his parents and they came at a run, Julia's eyes widening in consternation as she caught sight of the inert form of her daughter just inside the doorway.

"What happened, Nick? Did she trip and bang her head?"

"Not as far as I could see. She simply went down like a ton of bricks."

"I'm sure it's nothing to worry about," Gavin said soothingly, slipping an arm under his daughter's shoulders to support her head. "The journey was probably too much for her, so soon after the exams."

"But she's never fainted in her life!"

"She has now."

"I wish Hilary was here!" Julia said distractedly. "She'd know what to do."

"There's no need to do anything. Look, she's coming round already."

Vanessa moved her head suddenly and muttered something.

"What did she say?" Julia bent closer.

"Didn't catch it. Sounded like gibberish anyway."

The girl's eyes flickered then opened wide, fastening not on the faces of her family grouped about her but beyond and above them, and instinctively the rest of them turned and stared as well. A few feet away stood their inherited daily help, and although the seeming suddenness of her appearance could be accounted for by their absorption in Vanessa, each of them in turn felt a small jolt of unease. But the woman wasn't looking at any of them. Her pale eyes were fixed unwinkingly on Vanessa with an expression of almost fanatical excitement.

Gavin collected himself first. "How do you do, Mrs Hare? As you see, our daughter's had a fainting spell. Probably the long journey and the heat in the car. Unfortunately there's no bed she can lie on while she recovers."

With an effort the woman wrenched her eyes from the girl. "There's a wide window-seat in the dining-room, sir. If you pad it with a coat or something –"

Vanessa struggled to sit up and her father supported her. "I don't want to lie down. I'll be all right if I just sit in the car for a few minutes."

Julia regarded her anxiously. "Do you remember what happened, darling?"

"No, I felt fine right up to the minute I fell." She frowned and flexed her fingers. "I've got pins and needles, in my feet as well."

Through the open door the rumbling approach of the furniture vans reached them and Gavin straightened. "Take her back to the car then, will you, Nick, while I get things organized here."

For the next twenty minutes or so Vanessa leaned back against the cushions of the car seat watching through the open windows as piece after piece of furniture was unloaded and carried through the door which had proved such an impenetrable barrier to her. Ridiculous to pass out like that, completely without warning. And then, when she came round, to see that rather odd woman standing there –

The tingling in hands and feet intensified at the memory and, tired of the confines of the car, she climbed out again. Her head was aching slightly and she had no wish to become entangled in the procession of chair and chests which were now being unloaded. Instead, she turned away from the house and walked along the path leading round to the back garden.

A wide lawn sloped away from her up the side of the hill above the house, and amid the clover of the overgrown grass bees hummed contentedly. To her right a high hedge encircled quite a thriving kitchen garden, and a stone terrace ran along the back of the house. From the open windows she could hear the clatter and bang of heavy furniture and the sound of the men's voices as they guided each other through the doorways. She decided to explore the garden before the house. At least her first step here hadn't produced instant oblivion.

Hoping no-one would glance out of the window and call her back to her neglected duty, she set off up the lawn. At the far end three little paths led off invitingly between head-high hedges like the maze at Hampton Court. They provided an agreeable sense of privacy and Vanessa turned first along the left-hand one. It finished a few yards farther on in a little paved square in the centre of which stood a sundial with an old wooden bench alongside it, overhung with sweet-smelling honeysuckle. It would offer a lovely, private corner to escape to, provided Nick or Hilary didn't get here first. Well satisfied with her initial exploration, she retraced her steps and tried next the right-hand path, leading away diagonally opposite to the sundial. This proved equally rewarding, revealing a small wooden summer-house. Vanessa climbed up the uneven steps and rubbed a circle in the dirty glass of a window. She could not see much inside: an old table with a broken leg, and a sagging deck-chair. She tried the door, but it was locked.

Probably its key would be among the others belonging to the house.

Finally, having retraced her steps again, she started up the last central path, but here an unexpected obstruction awaited her. Round the first bend a large pile of sticks and branches had been erected, effectively blocking the way ahead.

Vanessa examined both sides of the barrier, but they had been carefully worked into the hedges lining the path and would not easily be pulled away. The solidity of the barricade increased her curiosity to know what lay beyond it, and she began systematically pulling away branches in the weakest central portion, scratching arms and legs as she did so. Five minutes later she had made a gap just large enough to squeeze through, and this she promptly did.

The path she was now following proved longer than the other two, twisting and turning every few feet until only by the position of the sun could she judge that it was in fact weaving a zigzag course for the far boundary wall at the highest point of the garden. Yet when at last she rounded the final bend she came to an abrupt halt, feeling the breath leave her body as an eerie sense of *déjà vu* washed over her. For ahead of her, dank and damp in its permanent shadows, squatted an ancient stone well, and she knew beyond doubt that it was this she had set out to find: this, and what still lay a little way beyond ...

Scarcely aware of what she was doing she walked slowly towards it, her hands going out of their own accord to caress the worn stone. But something was not as it should be. Painfully her eyes refocused and she saw that the top of the well had been boarded over. With a sense of urgency she began to pull and tug at the heavy wood but it was nailed down and would not move. It would be necessary to return tomorrow with the correct tools. She turned sharply, as though a voice had called her, and saw for the first time the gate in the garden wall leading out on to the hill. Her fingers were shaking as she pulled back the heavy bolts and the gate creakingly swung open on rusty hinges. Without thought she went through it on to the hillside above the garden. Here the breeze was stronger and she lifted her head to it like an animal and started up the slope, her heart beating rapidly in unacknowledged anticipation. A ten-minute climb brought her out on level ground at the top of the hill and for the second time in half an hour the sight that met her was what she had known it would be. Alone and magnificent in the deserted landscape, the primeval stone which towered before her seemed to dominate the entire world.

Vanessa went towards it as though to a magnet, hands outstretched and eyes glowing, and circled it three times, head tilted back to see the outline of it against the deep unbroken blue of the sky. It stood about fifteen feet high but at one side a jagged piece must have broken off at some time, leaving what looked like a narrow stone table some five feet in length. And instinctively Vanessa Prior, a child of the twentieth century, laid herself along it as sacrifices had been laid at regular intervals since time immemorial. And at the moment of contact an electrical shockwave, many times stronger than the 'pins and needles' she'd been aware of since arriving at Conningley, shuddered through her body, and for the second time that day consciousness slipped away from her.

How long she lay there she had no idea, and when she eventually stirred and sat up it was to find that her watch had stopped. Odd: she must have fallen asleep. The sun was almost directly overhead – and it seemed a long time since breakfast. Carefully she manoeuvred herself off her improvised stone bed, aware of subdued excitement, a promise of power and strange things to come. She paused to run her hand caressingly over the rough, sun-warmed stone and strange words came into her head: words which seemed vaguely familiar but which she couldn't understand.

"I'll be back," she said softly, and set off down the hill

again, through the garden gate which she carefully bolted behind her, past the impassive well and so through the gap in the barrier, emerging at the top of the lawn to see her family standing anxiously on the terrace below.

"There she is!"

Guiltily she started to run towards them. "Were you looking for me? I'm sorry."

"Where on earth were you?" Nick demanded. "I searched everywhere! Mum was convinced you'd passed out somewhere. Didn't you hear us calling?"

"No, I – I think I must have fallen asleep in the sun. I'm sorry," she said again, placatingly.

"Well, since you seem to be all right, never mind," her father said briskly. "The point is that the men are having their lunch break and it seemed a good idea to take ours too. There's a little pub down on the corner, if you'll settle for a ploughman's snack."

"As long as it's a big one! I'm ravenous!"

"That's a relief! I was beginning to wonder if you really were off-colour. You're certainly pale today."

"I'm fine." She gave a little skip of pure happiness. "I think I'm going to enjoy living here," she said.

"I can't say I've taken to the new daily," Gavin remarked half an hour later as they sat in the shade of an umbrella in the pub garden.

Julia reached for the salt. "Why, what's wrong with her? She's neat and tidy and almost pathologically anxious to be of help."

"Pathologically's right!"

"Her name suits her, anyway," Nick said through a mouthful of pickled onion. "With her large, flat eyes and that mousy hair scraped back, she looks exactly as a hare would if it were humanized! She even walks with a kind of lope!"

"Oh Nick, really!" his mother protested.

"It's true! Didn't people once believe that hares were

witches in disguise? Perhaps the reverse is true too! And the way she stood gloatingly over Van when she passed out – well, it gave me the willies, I can tell you!"

"As a matter of fact, I agree," Gavin said surprisingly. "I can't say I feel particularly comfortable when she suddenly materializes behind me!"

"That's it exactly, Dad! It's what she does! You never hear her coming. One moment she's not there, the next she is."

"Personally," remarked Julia, draining her glass of lager, "I think you're both being perfectly ridiculous. Poor woman, all she's done is try to be helpful." She paused and looked across at her daughter who had sat silently throughout the exchange. "What do you think, Vanessa? Did she strike you as odd in any way?"

"I've hardly seen her," the girl answered slowly. "Though I did get a strange kind of feeling –"

"What?"

"That it was she who brought me round when I fainted."

"But she wasn't anywhere near you!"

"No, I know."

"There you are, Mum! Three to one says she's a weirdo!"

"Weirdo or not," his mother retorted, "she has a willing pair of hands and I assure you I shall be making full use of them. Come on now, it's time we were getting back."

Nick stood up suddenly. "Look at that glider! That's the third I've seen; there must be a club round here. Can I learn gliding, Dad? It must be a fantastic sensation!"

"All in good time," Gavin said equably. "We have more pressing things to talk about at the moment. Back to work, everyone!"

In his office ten miles away in Aylesbury, Brian Cresswell had been thinking of the Priors at intervals throughout the day. It would be very pleasant to have them as neighbours again after a gap of five years. It might even help Marion;

she and Julia had been very close at one time. It was an incredible stroke of luck that he should have seen that house advertised for sale on the very day he learned Gavin was being moved back to Buckinghamshire. As a result of his phone call, Gavin and Julia had flown down the following day and put in an immediate offer for the house which, rather to their surprise, was accepted at once without any of the expected bargaining. Furthermore, the previous owners were almost embarrassingly eager to be accommodating, offering to move out at the earliest opportunity and even, so Julia laughingly informed him over the phone, bequeathing her their own cleaning woman! If he believed in such things, Brian told himself with a smile, it would have seemed that fate had specifically earmarked that house for the Priors.

And perhaps, as the thought came to him, there was malignant laughter in unholy places, for it was indeed a cruel twist of fate which used Brian to bring the Priors to Conningley and thereby ensure his own destruction.

At five-thirty as he left the office he decided to call on them briefly before going home. It would only add a few miles to his journey. He wouldn't stay, of course – just wish them well in their new home.

With this in mind he called at a greengrocer's for a basket of fruit. Flowers would hardly be welcome at this juncture – Julia wouldn't have time to arrange them – and he couldn't arrive empty-handed.

Five years, he thought as he took the Stoke Manderville road out of town. The children would have changed beyond recognition – Hilary engaged and within sight of being a qualified doctor, for heaven's sake! And little Van, his favourite, almost a young lady. How old would she be? Fifteen? Gavin had mentioned O-levels, and Nick taking his A's. At least, he thought with a rare touch of bitterness, not having a family did mean one wasn't quite so aware of the relentless passage of time.

Good for Julia – she'd got the curtains up already! He

stopped alongside Gavin's car to the right of the front door. The door itself still stood open and he tapped on it, pressed the bell lightly, and called,

"Anyone at home?"

There was a clatter of feet on the stairs and Vanessa – unmistakably Vanessa, with her hair still flying and, thank God, not a trace of make-up – came hurtling down and flung herself into his arms.

"Uncle Bran! Oh, Uncle Bran!"

He'd forgotten the baby name she'd always used but he held her close and shut his eyes on a spasm of pain. He'd have given a lot for a daughter like this. Smilingly he held her away from him.

"Let me look at you! Well, Van, thank goodness you haven't changed that much! Taller, of course – much – but still the little girl whose hair I used to brush when we came for dinner at Haddenham!"

She was smiling shyly under his scrutiny as Julia came hurrying from the back of the hall. "Brian? Is that you? How wonderful to see you! Do come in. Oh!" Her eyes fell on the basket of fruit he'd set down on the floor. "How perfectly sweet of you! We've none in the house and I didn't think of it till after the shops had shut."

He kissed her cheek. "Still as youthful as ever, Julia! I don't know how you do it!"

"Well, you should! Plenty of exercise has always been my motto! Just like –" She broke off and coloured and he put a hand quickly on her arm.

"It's all right, love. Don't worry about it."

"But I was going to be so careful," she said ruefully. "And then, in the very first sentence –"

"Forget it. And I won't come in now, really. I know how busy you must be. I only called to leave this and wish you much happiness in your new home."

"What's this about not coming in?" Gavin appeared and seized his friend's hand. "Great to see you, Brian. And we won't take 'no' for an answer. You must just excuse the chaos and come and drink a toast with us, to the Priors at Conningley!"

They'd hardly changed at all, Brian thought thankfully as he followed Gavin through the doorway. Julia was as slim and attractive as he remembered, even if her arms and legs were now rather muscular after all those years of conscientious exercise. As for Gavin, his thick grey hair and jutting chin still reminded Brian of the archetypal cavalry officer in films of the American Civil War. It was wonderful to have them back again.

The sitting-room, running right through the house, looked surprisingly normal. As Brian had noted there were curtains at the window, albeit makeshift ones, and rugs on the floor. There were even chairs to sit on and glasses to drink from. Brian dutifully raised his.

"The Priors at Conningley! Welcome back to Bucks! We've missed you."

Julia leaned forward. "Brian – how is Marion?"

His face clouded. "Much the same," he said evasively.

"I do hope we can help in some way. Once we get sorted out you must bring her to dinner."

He shook his head. "I'm afraid that wouldn't be feasible, Julia. We – don't go out to dinner any more."

"But – I thought if she had a wheel-chair –"

"She has, but most of the time she refuses to use it. In any case, she has to lie almost flat in it. She – can't feed herself, you see."

Julia's lips trembled. "Oh God – I didn't realize –"

Gavin said quietly, "What happened exactly? Do you mind talking about it?"

"No, of course not." Brian looked down at his hands gripping the glass. "You know how she was – mad on every kind of sport – squash, tennis, riding. Like you, Julia. That was one of the main things you had in common, wasn't it? One day she took the horse out – it was autumn and had been raining heavily. The ground was treacherous with wet leaves. The horse slipped, threw her and – rolled on top of her. Her spine was broken."

Gavin cleared his throat. "And that was – what – about three years ago?"

"Three and a half, yes."

"And there's been no improvement since?"

"None, and I don't think there will be. Nor does she." He straightened. "However, I didn't come to put a blight on your first evening in your new home. Let's talk of more cheerful things. What have you all been doing since we saw you?" He turned to Nick, who had come in during the last conversation and was standing grave-faced just inside the door. "You've just finished your A-levels, I believe? How long do they keep you in suspense?"

"Till the middle of August. Ghastly, isn't it? I intend to put the whole thing out of my mind for the next couple of months."

"Then university?"

"If I get the right grades, yes."

"And Vanessa, of course, has just finished her O-levels." Julia smiled across at her younger daughter. "She worked very hard for them – I hope it hasn't taken too much out of her. She hasn't seemed quite herself today."

"Well, at least you have an extra long summer holiday to compensate! Where's Hilary? Isn't she with you?"

"She's in Italy at the moment with one of her hospital friends," Julia told him. "She'll be joining us next weekend."

Brian set down his glass. "Now I really must be going. Marion worries if I'm at all late. In fact – is the phone connected? Perhaps I could just ring through and ask Miss Fergusson to tell her I'm on my way."

"Miss Fergusson?"

"The nurse. She lives in. God knows how I'd manage without her."

"I'll show you the phone," Gavin said quietly. Having left Brian to make his call he came back into the room and noticed that Vanessa's eyes were full of tears. In passing he laid his hand briefly on the blonde head.

"Poor Uncle Bran," she said brokenly. "And poor Auntie Marion. Imagine lying in bed *for ever!*"

Brian put his head round the door. "O.K., I'll be on my way. Thanks for the drink. May I tell Marion you'll be round to see her, Julia?"

"Of course – as soon as I possibly can."

"Fine. Good-bye, then."

He'd embarrassed them, he thought ruefully as he drove round the green and back on to the main road. There were certain taboos in even the most civilized families and unfortunately serious illness – or more accurately in this case, permanent paralysis – was one of them. Still, they would have to have faced it sooner or later and perhaps now the ground was cleared they'd all be able to be freer with each other. For himself, he was now able to view the situation with philosophical acceptance. Ironically, he had been helped by the fact that he and Marion had not loved one another for years. It was his secret that immediately prior to the accident he had been on the point of asking for a divorce: not because of love for anyone else, but simply because the constant bickering and general sterility of their marriage frustrated him.

Still, he could at least be thankful that the physical limitations his wife's accident had imposed on their marriage did not trouble him as much as his friends and acquaintances appeared to suppose. He had never regarded himself as a particularly physical man, though he was aware that his appearance – the broad shoulders, strong features, above all, perhaps, the beard he affected – pointed to the contrary. He had little patience with those of his acquaintances who involved themselves in unsavoury attachments, and prided himself on the fact that willpower and self-discipline enabled him to suppress the very occasional longings which his wife could no longer satisfy and which he was both too proud and too shy to seek to gratify elsewhere.

It might well have been this rather smug complacency which in the end caused his undoing.

The brief June darkness had fallen at last. At Conningley the downstairs lights flicked out as its exhausted new owners went thankfully to bed. But on the hillside above the shadowed garden a figure moved stealthily, making its way up the slope to the impassive shape of the Druid Stone, a black wedge against the paler darkness of the moonless sky.

Softly, reverently, Gerda Hare knelt at the stone altar where, hours earlier, Vanessa had lain, and, reaching up, carefully emptied milk from the jug she carried into a natural indentation in the surface of the stone. Her lips were moving in an ancient, mechanical ritual, but her mind, detached, was reviewing the far-reaching events of the day just gone. She alone had heard – and understood – the strange words with which Vanessa Prior had come out of her trance. Celtic they were, their origins lost in the dark wraiths of prehistory, but they had been spoken through the ages by the Priests and Priestesses of the Stone: 'I come to serve'.

And that service would soon be called for. The cycle was coming round again, as inexorably as the planets moved across the sky. Very soon now the Stone would awaken from its century-long sleep and demand appeasement.

Well satisfied, Gerda Hare inclined her head three times in the time-honoured obeisance. Then, careful not to turn her back to it, she retreated slowly and cautiously until the rim of the hill hid the Stone from her sight and she could turn and hurry down the slope to her cottage down on the main road.

Two

During that first week Julia was uncomfortably aware of putting off making the necessary visit to Marion. It was true that she was extremely busy, that the hours rushed past and there was not enough time in one day to do a quarter of the things which needed to be done. At the same time, she knew deep inside herself that if she really wanted to see her friend she would fit it in at the cost of leaving some other task undone. She also knew that each evening, when Gavin arrived home and enquired how the day had gone, he was waiting to be told about Marion. Not that he ever mentioned her. Nor did Julia, but the omission was causing a restraint between them which added to her guilty irritation.

"Nick's not being much help," she remarked crossly one evening. "He seems to spend most of his time hanging round the Glider Club up on the hill."

"What would you like him to do?"

"Just be here occassionally, when I need him. He could have saved me several dashes into Aylesbury and Wendover."

"Well, have you told him? He can hardly be expected to know if you're suffering in silence."

She flicked her cigarette lighter impatiently. "And Vanessa wanders round the place in a dream. Do you know what she was doing the other day? Prising up the wooden cover on the old well at the top of the garden!"

"I didn't even know there was one."

"Well there is, and the Dentons must have boarded it up for some reason. Anyway, nothing would satisfy her until it was open to the sky. Believe me, the stench of that stagnant water was overpowering. No wonder she still hasn't got her colour back."

"Tell her to keep away from it then, if it worries you." He eyed her over his glass. "It strikes me, my love, that you're a bit fraught. Don't try to do too much all at once. There's no hurry, goodness knows. The house is perfectly comfortable already without the myriad and one improvements you're aiming for!"

"But we can't have people round till we've sorted out the curtains, at least! And the dining-room wallpaper's ghastly! I don't want anyone to see it till it's been decorated."

"Who's likely to see it, for heaven's sake?"

"Well, the Pembrooks and all our Haddenham friends. Didn't I tell you that Linda phoned yesterday? She wants me to have a game of squash with her, but at the moment I just can't spare the time. She said she'd ring again in about ten days and fix a 'welcome back' party for us. And of course she mentioned that everyone's longing to see the house."

Gavin sighed and went to refill his glasss. "They can either see it as it is or wait until we're ready to do something about it. I've no intention of letting you work yourself into a decline for the sake of Linda Pembrook."

But talk of Linda had brought Marion to both their minds. She had been an inevitable companion in the past on visits to the squash club, and, goaded at last into making some statement of intent, Julia said abruptly,

"All right. I'll go and see her tomorrow."

A casual listener would have assumed she was still referring to Linda, but Gavin knew better. He nodded and wisely refrained from comment.

Vanessa walked slowly back down the central path towards the lawn. There was no longer any trace of the barrier of branches she had encountered the first time. Their removal had been her first priority the day after they moved into the house. From the top of the lawn she could see over the hedge into the kitchen garden, where Mrs Hare, a basket on her arm, was collecting the day's crop of broad beans.

Vanessa hesitated. She had not forgotten her brother's comments and to a large extent she agreed with them, yet some sense of curiosity drew her to the woman. There was something in the way she went about her work that intrigued the girl; almost as though, while doing it to the best of her ability, she regarded it simply as the means to an end, and Vanessa found herself wondering what that end could be.

These reflections had carried her down the grass and round the hedge into the vegetable garden. Mrs Hare went on with her quick plucking without turning round.

"Good morning, Miss."

"Good morning." Something further seemed called for, and she added, "Can I help?"

"Bless you no, Miss. Won't take me two minutes to finish them." She did turn her head then, and Vanessa found the darting glance of those pale, flat eyes oddly disconcerting. "Been paying your respects to the Stone, have you dearie?"

The girl started. "I – have been up there, yes. It's very – impressive, isn't it?"

"Oh, it's impressive, right enough. You can understand folk worshipping it, can't you? In the old days, I mean."

"Is it very old?"

"Lordie yes. At least five thousand years, they reckon."

"Five *thousand*?" Vanessa stared at her wide-eyed.

"Long before the Romans came." Mrs Hare smiled slightly, her fingers still picking the young beans and dropping them into her basket. "Legend has it the Stone climbed up to the top of the hill there by itself. Like them Rollright Stones, over in Oxfordshire." She paused, then added matter-of-factly, "It's grateful to you for uncovering the well, dear."

There didn't seem to be any possible reply to that, so

Vanessa didn't attempt one. Mrs Hare glanced at her again and gave a short laugh, leaving the girl uncertain whether or not she had meant the remark seriously. To cover her confusion she bent forward and snapped a bean from the nearest row, slitting it with her thumb nail and popping one of the sweet, tender beans into her mouth.

"Has it got a name?" she asked suddenly.

"It's shown as the Druid Stone on all the maps but folk hereabouts have another name for it. They call it the Screeching Stone."

Vanessa was unable to suppress an involuntary shudder. "That sounds rather scarey!" she said, with an attempt at a laugh. Her eyes were fixed on the woman's swiftly moving fingers – snapping and tossing, snapping and tossing, forming an arc of continuous movement.

"They say that in the old days it was used as an altar – for sacrifices, you know." The eyes which fastened on her were large and liquid, like an animal's. "And when the sacrifice had been made and the Stone's thirst was quenched, it gave out a high-pitched screech. People used to hide away and listen for it and not come out till they heard it and knew they were safe again."

"People?" whispered Vanessa fearfully. "They sacrificed *people*?"

"Well, it was very long ago, like," Mrs Hare said apologetically. But Vanessa had heard enough.

"I must go in," she said in a rush, and turned and ran from the garden. Mrs Hare stood looking after her, her fingers still at last, and there was a faint, satisfied smile on her lips.

It was a perfect summer afternoon and there were a hundred things Julia should have been doing instead of driving along these glorious country roads. But gradually the warm sunshine and the richness of the pastures spreading on either side began to soothe her and she drew a long, quivering breath. Perhaps it wouldn't be too bad after all, though this first visit was bound to be the most difficult.

Her thoughts moved backwards and she tried to think of the last occasion she had driven this way. It must have been shortly before their departure to Newcastle, when she'd come to say good-bye. Almost impossible to think herself back into that self of five years ago, when the children were so much younger: Vanessa only ten, with a high pony-tail and a brace on her teeth and Hilary just deciding she wanted to make medicine her career.

How familiar the road seemed now as she approached the village, and as she turned into the well-remembered gateway it was hard to believe that Marion would not this time – or ever again – come hurrying to meet her.

There'd always been a housekeeper, of course. Marion wasn't the domestic type and the woman had been in her family for years. There was an obscure comfort in recognizing the face which confronted her as the door opened.

"Good afternoon, Mrs Hanbury. I've called to see Mrs Cresswell."

"Yes, of course. Mrs Prior, isn't it? Nice to see you again, ma'am, even if it has to be in these sad circumstances." Ready tears came to the woman's eyes and she dabbed at them ineffectually.

"How – how is she?" Julia asked awkwardly.

"Never varies, poor lamb. But she'll be pleased to see you. I'll take you straight up."

It was all so unnervingly the same – the dark blue carpet with the exotic flowers on it, the Constable print in the hall. Steeling herself, Julia followed the ample hips of Mrs Hanbury up the shallow stairs. At the remembered door she stopped and knocked. Julia listened for Marion's voice, but instead there was a rustle of starched skirts and the door opened to reveal a small thin woman in nurse's uniform.

"This is Mrs Prior, Nurse, an old friend of Madam's," Mrs Hanbury said in a low voice. "They've just come back to the district."

"Ah yes, Mrs Cresswell mentioned you, Mrs Prior." The voice was brisk and heavily Scottish. "Come away in."

With her head high and the flowers she had brought clasped like a talisman, Julia went into the room. The first thing that struck her was that the bed was different, a special orthopaedic one. Of course, Brian would have had to move to another room, she thought confusedly.

"Well, Julia! It's been a long time!" The same voice, firm, slightly mocking, leaving Julia uncomfortably wondering whether she was referring to the past five years or five days.

"Marion dear!" She bent down swiftly and kissed her cheek. What in heaven's name did she say next? she wondered in a panic.

Behind her the condescending Scots voice said, "I'll leave you two ladies to have a wee chat and be back shortly with some tea. And if you'll give me those lovely flowers, Mrs Prior dear, I'll put them in a vase."

Julia thrust them at her blindly and the door closed behind her.

Marion said through clenched teeth, "God help me, that woman will be the death of me!"

The unexpected but completely natural remark broke the ice. Julia laughed and pulled up a chair, reaching for her friend's hand. "Oh Marion, what can I say?"

"Nothing, my dear, positively damn-all. It's all been said countless times, including in your own letters. Let's take it as read." She paused, then added gently, "Don't be afraid to look at me, Julia. You're bound to be curious and it'll only lead to embarrassment if you try to hide it. Look and ask all you want to, then we can forget it."

Julia's eyes went slowly to the well-known face, thinner now, the eyes slightly sunken with pain, but the bright chestnut hair as springy and curling as ever. The almost useless arms laid over the coverlet were thin and white where they had used to be strong and muscular, slamming balls to the base line, carving a way through the water in the swimming-pool.

Julia said in a whisper, "Is the pain very bad?"

"Well, it's not continuous, put it that way. Hell, Julia, I *know* I've a lot to be thankful for: enough money to be looked after comfortably in my own home, special gadgets to enable me to speak on the phone, switch on the television, even turn the pages of books –"

She flung her head to one side and with appalled pity Julia saw her struggling to keep her lip from trembling. "But – well – sometimes I can't help wondering whether it was worth the long fight back. Is that very wicked of me, when you think what my life used to be and how it is now? I'm not a good invalid, I'm the first to admit it. Sometimes I let fly and rant and scream against fate and everybody who happens to be in the vicinity. And that infernal woman comes and sponges my face and says reprovingly, 'We are in a paddy today, aren't we?'"

She gave a shuddering laugh and turned back to Julia, her eyes bright with unshed tears. "You probably know me as well as anyone does. Can't you imagine the state I get into sometimes, knowing that patience has never been my strong suit?"

"Of course I can, and I'm sure it's necessary for you to let off steam. Oh Marion, if only there was something I could do!"

"There is. You can tell me from time to time that I'm an ungrateful bitch and to shut up and count my blessings. That's what I need, you know, but all I get is sweet reason on all sides – poor old Daisy Hanbury, Miss Fergusson, Brian – particularly Brian. God, I make his life hell, Julia. I spend my time trying to needle him into losing his temper. I'd feel so much better if he'd lash out at me occasionally but of course he never will. The world's most civilized man, that's my husband!"

She looked up suddenly. "Am I shocking you after all?"

"No, but – well, try not to be too hard on him. His whole

life has changed too."

Marion said softly, "You know, I had the feeling, just before the accident, that he was screwing up his courage to ask me for a divorce. I wouldn't have had any objection, either. We'd never been lovey-dovey like you and Gavin, you know that, but things had been going from bad to worse. How he must have wished we'd made the break before this happened and tied us irrevocably together! Of course, I did offer him his freedom afterwards, and I meant it sincerely, but you can imagine his reaction. His schoolboy code of ethics just wouldn't let him grab it and get the hell out. Sometimes I almost wish he had."

There was a tap on the door. "Back to buns and banalities!" Marion said under her breath, and Julia had to hide her smile as she pulled forward a table for Miss Fergusson to set down the tray.

"Anyway, Julia," Marion began, when the distressing business of giving her a drink and some fingers of hot-buttered toast had been accomplished, "we've been talking about me all this time, and I want to hear about you. How is everyone? Is Hilary as gorgeous as ever? Tell me about this lucky young man she's going to marry."

"Well, he's a doctor too, of course. They met at medical school. He was a year ahead of her and they were virtually inseparable for the last couple of years."

"I was surprised when Brian told me she was hoping to come down here for her year as house officer."

Julia smiled. "You do sound knowledgeable! I usually have to explain—" She broke off and flushed.

"Quite so," Marion said dryly. "I should, shouldn't I? There's been no shortage of doctors in my life over the last three years. But to return to my point, I'd have expected her to want to stay up in Newcastle with him."

"But you see he's not there at the moment. He was offered the chance of a year in Africa studying tropical diseases, which have apparently always interested him. They talked it over carefully and decided he should go."

"And became engaged just before he left? Wasn't that a little short-sighted?"

Julia shrugged. "I suppose they felt it was a form of insurance, cementing their relationship before the enforced separation."

"How long has he been gone now?"

"Only since April. She was completely desolate at first, but I can't help suspecting that a large proportion of it was simply habit. Personally I think this year apart is the best thing that could have happened. If they still want to marry when he comes back, then I shan't have any doubts either. And if they don't – well, there's no real harm done."

"I hope if she does get married next year she won't promptly start a family and let all that expensive training go to pot."

"I don't think she'll do that, though of course she wants a family eventually."

"Of course!" Marion echoed ironically.

Julia smiled. "I'm not going to be drawn into that old argument! You've stated your case many times before." But would life have been more bearable for Brian, she wondered privately, if Marion hadn't been so adamantly against having children? She had always felt, though he'd never said as much, that he himself would have liked a family. And now, in the face of Marion's withdrawal, he had no outlet at all for his affections.

Marion's voice roused her from her musings. "And little Van – how is she? Growing up fast, I imagine?"

"Yes, she's quite tall for fifteen but she hasn't really changed much. She could do with putting a little weight on; I sometimes wonder if she isn't outgrowing her strength."

"Give her plenty of red meat, my dear, that's what's called for!" Miss Fergusson put in unexpectedly. "Young girls these days have their heads stuffed full of diets and such nonsense. Laying up trouble for the years ahead, I always say."

"Vanessa certainly doesn't diet," Julia answered mildly.

"In fact, she eats enough to satisfy a farm labourer, as her father continually points out! Still, I'll – remember the tip about the red meat." And she carefully avoided Marion's mocking eyes.

The tea-tray was cleared away and Julia rose to her feet. "I really must be getting back, Marion. I haven't even peeled the potatoes for the evening meal."

"Of course. I mustn't keep you. Next time I want to hear all about the house. Brian feels quite proprietorial about it, having as it were brought you together." She hesitated and added with an undercurrent of urgency, "You will come again, won't you, Julia?"

"Of course I shall." Impulsively she bent to kiss her. "And the girls will be coming too. They're anxious to see you. You'll have to watch out for Hilary, though. She's bound to have some way-out medical theory which will put you on your feet in no time!"

"If so, she'll have my full co-operation! Thanks for coming, Julia. I know it wasn't easy for you, but believe me I do appreciate it. Bless you."

The room blurred before Julia's eyes and she turned quickly away. "See you again soon!" she said brightly, and almost ran from the room.

She drove home rather too quickly, hurried straight into the kitchen and peeled the potatoes. She was slightly surprised to find she was trembling, and almost cut herself several times. Out on the terrace she could see the back of Nick's head, deep in a book. Oh, thank God for them! she thought suddenly; for Gavin and Nick and Hilary and Vanessa and for the fact that they were all so *well*! She dropped the knife with a little clatter and ran up to her room. There, after closing the door carefully behind her, she put her trembling hands to her face and said softly, "Oh, Marion!"

Then the tears came, trickling through her fingers and down her wrists and she was powerless to do anything to stop them. Gavin found her there when he came home ten minutes later and gathered her into his arms. For a long time he held her silently while the shuddering helpless sobs shook her body. Then, as her breathing began to quieten, he kissed her hair and spoke soothingly.

"My poor darling, was it very terrible? I was expecting something like this. That's why I left the office a little early."

"The appalling thing," Julia said between gasps, "is that it's still the same Marion, caged up in that helpless body. I think I'd fooled myself into believing all the comfortable clichés about suffering making saints, and so on. Heaven forgive me, I expected her to be all sweetness and light, nobly prepared to accept it all, and I was shocked – *shocked*, Gavin, when I found she wasn't. She's the same, straight-speaking person she's always been, not mincing matters, letting you have it between the eyes. She can't escape the facts, so why should you? That kind of attitude. If I'd really thought about it, I'd have known all along that was how she'd have to be. But with being away when it happened and for so long afterwards, I suppose my memory of her forcefulness had blurred a little – probably because I couldn't bear the thought of the real Marion in that terrible condition.

"Well, the blinkers were certainly ripped off today. Her old self came back into focus and I finally had to accept the full horror of what has happened to her."

"In other words, it's delayed shock, isn't it? Poor love, I'm sorry it proved so shattering. Still, at least she's in her own home, with a loving husband to care for her and every comfort."

"Yes." Julia detached herself from his arms and blew her nose. A loving husband: did that really describe Brian? Patient, yes. Caring, certainly. But loving? If it was true, as Marion suspected, that he'd been on the point of suggesting divorce when the catastrophe struck, could it be that he felt as trapped as she did, and possibly equally resentful? It was a new slant on her friend's marriage and one that she didn't particularly care for, but she wouldn't betray Marion's confidence by sowing doubts in Gavin's mind.

"Anyway," she said resolutely, putting away her handkerchief, "I know the facts now and they'll just have to be faced. Even if she's immobile, Marion's still an amusing companion and on the mental plane we've as much in common as we ever had. It won't be any hardship to see her regularly, and it may well be a salutary lesson for me, too."

She turned and looked at her husband. "Don't let's ever take things for granted," she said softly. "We have so much to be thankful for." She smiled slightly. "Sorry darling. End of homily! Now I'd better go down and see to the dinner."

Three

"Could I get that down for you? It looks heavy!"

Hilary turned, bracing herself against the back of the seat as the train slowed down for its approach to Wendover.

"Thank you, I'd be very grateful."

It was the man who'd joined the train a few stations down the line. She'd been aware of his occasional glances but had kept her eyes dutifully on her magazine.

"Just back from holiday, I see!" he added with a smile as he swung down the heavy case to disclose the airline label.

"Yes, three weeks in Italy."

"My favourite country!"

"You know it well?"

"Fairly, yes. I'm lucky enough to be able to claim business expenses on some of my visits!"

The train creaked to a stop and along its length doors banged as commuters hurried out on to the platform.

"Is anyone meeting you?" her companion asked.

"No, we changed to an earlier plane and I hadn't time to

phone from Marylebone. Will there be any taxis?"

"You might have to queue. Are you going far?"

"Quite a way, yes. To Ickfield."

"Now there's a coincidence – so am I! Perhaps I could give you a lift?" He caught her hesitation and grinned. "Or don't you accept lifts from strange men?"

She smiled back. "The way I feel now, I'd accept a lift from anyone! Sorry – that did sound ungracious!"

"I asked for it." They had crossed over the bridge and come out into the station approach. As he had anticipated, quite a long line of people was forming at the taxi rank. Her companion put down the case.

"If you'll just wait here a moment I'll get the car."

Hilary watched him walk briskly into the car park. He was tall and broad-shouldered, his dark blond hair cut straight across his forehead, and there was a humorous quirk to his mouth which she found attractive. But only academically, Chris! she added quickly in her head. Being engaged didn't necessarily make one blind, she realized.

The neat red sports car drew to a halt beside her and the case was tossed on to the back seat together with her hand luggage.

"I'd better introduce myself. My name's Adam Sandys – spelt 'ys' for some reason, but still pronounced 'Sands'."

"Hilary Prior."

He gave a mock bow as he held open the door. "How do you do? You know, I thought I had a pretty good idea of everyone who lived in Ickfield. I can't believe I could have overlooked you!"

"Actually, I haven't been there yet. My family moved down from Newcastle last week."

"Ah – Conningley? I heard it had changed hands again."

He had put on dark glasses against the strong sunshine and Hilary felt in her bag for her own.

"Thank goodness tomorrow's Saturday!" he added, inching out on to the road. "This isn't the weather for working!"

"Yours must be interesting work, though, if it takes you to Italy."

"Not all that often, I'm afraid. My parents run a string of antique shops, called, I hate to tell you, *Sandys of Time!* Father has these occasional bursts of whimsy and we couldn't talk him out of it! There are four or five shops dotted round the Chilterns and I move around between them."

The road had started to climb steeply. On their left, beyond the richly cultivated fields, the wooded hillside closed them in, while on the right the ground fell away, affording a magnificent view over the surrounding countryside. Sensing her tiredness, Adam Sandys lapsed into companionable silence and she was grateful. She'd forgotten how rich and varied the Buckinghamshire countryside could be, and the strains of the long day's travelling ebbed away as she let herself relax and enjoy it.

Just beyond Ellesborough, Adam turned to the left and for a while the going was very steep as the road cut its way like a tunnel through the enclosing woods. Then it levelled off slightly, veered to the right, and opened out again with fields and farms on either side. A signpost proclaimed 'Ickfield 2 miles'.

Adam glanced at her. "Do you know this part of the world?"

"Oh yes. We lived in Haddenham until five years ago and we've friends in Kimble."

"So it's back on home ground again. Here's Ickfield now."

More houses were springing up along the road, which turned sharply to the right opening up into a fairly wide High Street lined with interesting-looking old shops and houses.

"That's our place, conveniently situated next to the off-licence!"

Hilary caught a quick glimpse of a diamond-paned bow window with a piece of furniture gleaming richly behind it,

then, on the left, she saw the green and the duckpond her
parents had described. Adam circled the green and turned
into the driveway of the house standing above the road.

"I might as well take you right to the door!"

Julia was just coming round the side of the house from
the garage.

"Hilary! Darling, you're early! How lovely!"

Hilary scrambled out and kissed her. "Mother, this is
Adam Sandys. He was on the train and gave me a lift from
Wendover."

"How very kind. Have you any connection with the
antique shop in the village? I've been haunting it every
chance I've had!"

"Yes, indeed. I hope you find something of interest. Shall
I put the case in the hall for you?"

Julia held open the door. "Could we offer you a cup of
tea? I'm just about to make one."

"That would be extremely welcome."

"Nick and Vanessa are out on the terrace, Hilary. If
you'd like to take Mr Sandys through I'll bring the tea in a
moment or two."

It was pleasantly shady on the terrace now the sun had
moved off it and Hilary sat back in the deck-chair and let
her eyes move lazily up the slope of the garden to the
hillside above it.

"I hadn't realized we were actually perched on a
Chiltern, as it were!"

"What's more," Nick informed her, "we've one of those
odd standing stones just up the hill." He turned to Adam.
"I suppose as a long-term resident you know all about it?"

"The Druid Stone? Yes, it's quite famous, but if you're
interested in ancient monuments you have one even nearer
– in your own garden, in fact!"

"The well, you mean? Vanessa's always hanging round
it, but I didn't realize there was anything special about it."

"Oh yes. A lot of work was done on it a few years back
and some fantastic things were found, including the skull of

a young woman which was about two thousand years old."

Vanessa, who had been watching him intently, gave a little shudder. "You mean she was drowned in it?"

"I doubt it. It was more likely to be tied up with the Celtic cult of the head. It was common practice, for instance, to behead your enemies and throw their heads into wells or streams. They believed that it somehow affected the property of the water."

"I imagine that it would!" Hilary commented dryly.

Adam smiled. "I mean they believed a '*tête coupée*' as it's called could promote healing properties in a well."

"'*Tête coupée*'?" echoed Julia, coming out with the tray. "That sounds pretty gruesome!"

"We're talking about the well, Mum. Adam says it's very old."

"Really? Perhaps that's why the water smells so bad!"

"Back to the severed head!" Nick grinned. "But actually before we got on to the well I was going to tell you something about the Stone." He glanced up at his mother. "Did you know there's one on the hill?"

"A monument, you mean? I haven't actually had time to explore."

"I've only seen it myself in the distance, when I was up watching the gliding, but I heard something rather odd this afternoon which whetted my interest. A woman came into the post office with a little boy clinging to her for dear life. He wouldn't even let go of her hand for her to get her purse out. The woman behind the counter asked what was wrong and his mother said he'd been up on the hill with his brother and wandered off by himself. Apparently his brother suddenly heard him screaming, and when he rushed over to see what was wrong, the kid said the Stone had hit him!"

"The *Stone*?" Hilary repeated incredulously.

"Yes. I thought at first he meant someone had thrown a stone at him, but it wasn't that. According to his mother, he said he was over by the big Stone when he saw 'a huge bunny' sitting looking at him. I suppose it must have been a hare. Anyway, he started to chase it, apparently, and then he insists that the Stone hit him, because it didn't want him to catch 'the bunny'! What do you make of that? He certainly had quite a nasty bruise on the side of his head."

"He probably tripped and banged his head against it," commented Hilary.

Vanessa said expressionlessly, "Mrs Hare says people used to be sacrificed to the Stone."

"Mrs Hare would! Gosh – I never thought of that! It was probably her the kid saw up there, in her *alter ego*!"

"Who on earth is Mrs Hare?" Hilary asked in bewilderment. "This conversation is rapidly getting beyond me!"

"She's Mum's spooky new help. Did she really tell you that, Van – that people were sacrificed?"

"It's probably true," Adam said quietly. "The name Druid has always been associated with the Stone, and human sacrifices were one of their specialities. Actually quite a few of the legends concerning it link up with your well. For instance, the Stone is supposed to come down and drink at the well on Midsummer Day!"

"Good Lord! That was last weekend, wasn't it? I wish I'd known; I'd have watched out for it!"

Vanessa sat very still. She could feel the sweat pouring down her body inside her T-shirt. *It's grateful to you for uncovering the well.* When was it she had removed the cover? Actually on Midsummer Day itself; just in time for the Stone to drink? For the first time she wondered uneasily why it had seemed so imperative, last Saturday morning, to go and lever up the wooden planks, even before she'd finished unpacking her case.

Hilary stood up purposefully. "This well I have to see! Come on, Van, show us where it is!"

In silence Vanessa led the way along the centre path between the small untidy hedges to the clearing against the far wall where the well stood, grey and secretive. Hilary peered into it rather dubiously.

"It's very deep, isn't it? I can hardly see the bottom. What else did they find in it?"

"Bones of all kinds," Adam replied. "Ox, horse, hog, and so on. And some Roman tiles and fragments of Bronze Age pottery."

"Quite a cache. Well, I don't envy the Stone its drinking water! No wonder it only comes once a year! Does that gate lead up on to the hill?"

Adam laughed. "Yes, and it wasn't put there, as you might imagine, for the convenience of the people who lived here but to ensure that the Stone still had access to the well! I remember reading that once, in an article about the village."

Julia shivered. "I can't imagine why you didn't leave the thing boarded up, Vanessa. It looks most unhealthy to me."

Adam looked at the girl with sudden interest. "You removed a cover of some sort? Why?"

She flushed. "It just seemed – wrong for it to be closed in, that's all." She turned and started to make her way back along the path and after a moment the others followed her. Obscurely she resented having to let them all peer into the well and make derogatory comments about it. She'd found it, and she'd uncovered it. It was hers – and the Stone's.

Back on the terrace Adam Sandys thanked them for the tea and prepared to leave. Hilary walked round the house with him.

"Thanks again for the lift. I probably shouldn't have been home yet if I'd had to wait for a taxi!"

"It was a pleasure. I hope we'll meet again. And do tell your mother to let me know if she'd like me to keep an eye open for anything special in the antique line."

"Thanks, I will."

She watched him drive out of the gate and went back to the terrace, where her mother was loading the tray. Julia looked up and smiled.

"Well, how was Italy?"

"Fabulous, but I'll tell you all about it over dinner, so everyone can hear. What time are we eating, by the way? Have I time for a bath?"

"Yes, of course. I'll come up with you and show you your room. By the way, there's a letter from Rokeby waiting for you, and a couple from Chris."

"Oh, Mother – where is it? Why didn't you tell me before? It'll be the consultant's decision about the job!"

"They're all on the hall table." Julia watched her musingly as she ran through the french windows. Chris's letters were obviously completely overshadowed by the one from the hospital, but perhaps that was only to be expected. A moment later Hilary reappeared, the opened letter in her hand.

"It's O.K. – they've accepted me! I start as house officer on the seventeenth. Oh, the relief! Rokeby was really my first choice. It's got an excellent reputation, and it's only just along the road. I must phone Sally and see if she's had her reply yet."

An hour later, when Julia glanced into her daughter's room, the two airmail letters still lay unopened on the bed.

"You're very quiet this evening, Adam." Louise looked at him speculatively over the rim of her glass.

He stirred and smiled across at her. "Sorry. I've had rather a tiring day."

"Oh yes. Didn't you say you'd promised the car to David before you realized you'd have to go to Amersham? Don't tell me it wasn't at the station waiting for you?"

"No, it was there all right, but it was a wasted journey anyway. The purchaser for the Regency sideboard has backed down, unfortunately."

"Too bad." She stretched. "My day was somewhat fraught, too. A couple of deadlines have passed without the articles forthcoming and press day looms ever nearer. I just hope to God they don't need too much subbing when they do arrive. One's on Venetian glass. Would you have time to glance at it, to make sure there aren't any glaring errors?"

"I imagine so." He put down his glass. "Can I get you anything else?"

"No, thanks. We might as well be going, mightn't we?"

Outside, the streets were still warm with the day's stored sunshine. They walked slowly, arm-in-arm, not speaking until Louise said suddenly,

"You're still preoccupied, aren't you? Are you sure you're only tired or is something worrying you?"

"Not really, no."

"You can tell me, you know, whatever it is."

He gave her arm a little squeeze. "I know I can."

"So?"

He smiled. "Persistent, aren't you?"

"Well, it's not like you. I've seen you tired before but not – abstracted, like this."

"I'm sorry. I've not been very good company this evening."

"Your mind's obviously on something else. Or someone." She stopped suddenly. "Is that it, Adam? Did some beautiful girl swim into your orbit in Amersham today?"

"I'm beginning to think," he said slowly, "that you know me too well. No –" at her exclamation – "you're only partly right. I did meet someone, though not in Amersham, and I haven't fallen madly in love with her. You can keep that line for your glossy magazine!"

"But all the same you're interested, aren't you? Come on, you can tell Auntie Lou!"

"Even if I were, there wouldn't be much future in it. She was wearing a rather prominent engagement ring."

"Who is she, anyway?"

"Her family has just moved to Ickfield. I ran her home from Wendover and met some of them. They seem very pleasant."

"And all this because you let David have the car today! Well, well!"

They had reached her block of flats and Adam's car was parked outside. "Are you coming in for a while?"

"I don't think so, thanks. For all your scepticism I really am tired."

She smiled, slipped her arms round his neck and closed her eyes to receive his kiss.

"I can't persuade you to change your mind?" she murmured against his lips.

"No, love, not tonight, really. For one thing there are some figures I must add up before I go to bed." He smiled down at her. "Let me know when you receive that article on glass and I'll vet it for you."

"All right. Thanks."

He waited while she turned the key in the lock, gave her a last kiss and turned to the car. Thoughtfully she went on up the stairs to her flat. Her friendship with Adam Sandys meant a great deal to her, but they had agreed at the beginning that it would have no strings. The arrangement had suited them both admirably, keeping off unwanted encroachers and asking no questions if an occasional encroacher should not prove unwanted. A year ago she had lost her head over one of the photographers working on a long-term feature and the affair, explosive and all-consuming, had lasted for three months before it burned itself out. Adam had waited quietly on the sidelines until, bruised and shaken, she'd returned to him and poured out the whole story. Then, patiently, he had helped her back on to an even keel.

She flicked on the light in the tiny hallway and went straight through to the bedroom, still thinking over their two years together, wondering how she would feel if they were now about to end. For although she herself was a career girl and the thought of marriage held no allure for her, she'd always known that sooner or later Adam would fall for some nice girl who'd be only too delighted to darn his socks and bear his children. In fact, there had been several already, and it was her good fortune that none of

them had really interested him. Somehow, though, she felt
that the girl he'd met today was different; that, engagement
ring or not, she was the first real threat to the no-strings
relationship.

Well, time would tell, and if the threat did materialise, no
doubt she would survive. Shaking herself out of her
retrospection, she started to undress.

Four

"Please, Marion," Julia said again. "We'd love you to come!
It would make a pleasant day out for both of you
and I'm sure you could do with a change of scene! You'd be
perfectly comfortable, surely, on the sitting-room sofa."

"Oh Julia, I don't know. The truth is I've rather lost my
nerve. Except for hospital visits I haven't been out of the
house for about a year."

"That's because you haven't had us to drag you out! I
really can't see what the problem is. Brian said you can
travel quite well in the car and you could bring the wheel-
chair to get you from there into the house. You needn't feel
embarrassed with us, you know us all far too well. Now,
you will come, won't you?"

"I know Brian would like to, but don't you think –?"

"We want both of you," Julia said firmly. "Right, that's
fixed, then. Come about twelve and after lunch we can all
have a lovely lazy afternoon together. All right?"

"All right," Marion said at last. "And – thank you."

Julia turned from the phone as Gavin came into the
room. "Brian and Marion are coming for lunch tomorrow."

"Well done. I never thought she'd agree, after what
Brian said."

"It was for Brian's sake as much as hers that I insisted. She did suggest he came without her, but he'd obviously have felt guilty. I imagine his social life has been virtually nil since the accident."

"That reminds me," Gavin remarked, "there's a Golf Club dinner next Friday, a strictly 'men only' affair. I'll ask Brian to come along with me – it might cheer him up a bit."

Vanessa put her head round the door. "When's lunch?"

"About one, I suppose. I haven't even thought about it."

"Can I have an apple, then, to put me on?"

"The amount you eat," her father commented, "should make you like the side of a house! There ain't no justice!" He ruffled her hair affectionately. "What have you been doing this morning?"

She pulled a face and perched on the arm of a chair. "Trying unsuccessfully to find myself a holiday job."

"Did you go to *Sandys of Time*?" Julia asked with a smile.

Gavin looked across at her. "Where?"

"The antique shop in the village. The owner's son ran Hilary home yesterday."

"No," Vanessa answered, "I thought it would be too specialized and I'd be terrified of dropping something. But I asked at the post office and the fruit shop and the bakery –"

Gavin gave a snort of laughter. "That's my girl! Confine your search to where food is readily to hand!"

She ignored him and went on, "– and the butcher and the supermarket place, but none of them have any vacancies. I suppose I'll have to try Wendover or Aylesbury, but then the fares would eat into my pay."

"I shouldn't bother about a job at the moment," Julia advised. "You've had a year's very hard work. Why not just relax for the summer, and perhaps find yourself a Saturday job when you go back to school?"

"Well, I'll see, but I don't know anyone round here and Nick's not much company. All he can think about is gliding."

Not that she was really bored, Vanessa reflected as she

went through to the dining-room and selected an apple from the fruit-bowl. She had bought a couple of Agatha Christie paperbacks at the post office and was looking forward to taking them up on the hill after lunch. Though she didn't analyse the thought, she realized subconsciously that she always felt restless until she had made her daily visit to the Stone.

Accordingly that afternoon, when her parents sat down with the papers and Hilary went up to her room to write to Chris, Vanessa collected her paperbacks and slipped quietly through the garden to the gate leading to the hillside. As always she was aware of an unaccountable spurt of excitement as she came over the brow of the hill and caught sight of the Druid Stone. It seemed to be waiting for her, like some huge prehistoric monster dozing in the sunshine. With a contented little sigh she settled herself with her back against its warm roughness and opened a book.

It was some time before she became aware of 'the others'. Once, she thought she caught a flicker of movement just beyond her vision and turned quickly, but there was nothing there. Then, although the Stone sheltered her from any breeze, the pages of her book kept closing as though unseen hands were trying to claim her attention. And finally she became aware of whispered murmurings, though whether or not they were inside her head she could not be sure.

She stirred uneasily and glanced about her, remembering Nick's story of the little boy who insisted that the Stone had hit him, yet she was not really alarmed. There was a sense of deep harmony between herself and the Stone and she knew she was in no danger. However, it seemed obvious that something somewhere was trying to communicate with her and, abandoning her attempt to read, she laid the book on the grass beside her and deliberately emptied her mind to receive whatever message was waiting for her.

Immediately, as though sluice-gates had been opened, a

torrent of impressions, dreams and ideas flooded her consciousness and totally submerged it in a whirling, drowning eddy of confusion, overpowering her brief, instinctive struggle and ruthlessly sucking her under.

Time disintegrated, shifted, came together in a different form. Seeming to float through dense atmosphere, Vanessa found herself stretched once more on the altar slab while strange stories unfolded themselves in her head, sometimes in an archaic form of English and sometimes in a language which, though she didn't recognize, she had no difficulty in understanding: stories of mythical birds and beasts, of gods and goddesses, warriors and ladies, stories which, though a part of her ancestral heritage, had a special message for her alone: *We who have gone before have served the Stone. So, now, must you.*

"Van! What on earth are you doing there?"

As her eyes came fully open her misty companions vanished and she lay staring dazedly at the pitted surface of the stone, feeling its bumps and ridges pressing painfully into her cheek.

"Van! Wake up!"

Awkwardly she raised her head to see Nick standing staring at her with a mixture of impatience and incomprehension. "What a place to choose for a nap! You've a groove right across your face from lying on that thing! Why didn't you lie on the grass?"

With an effort she swung her legs to the ground, glancing down at her watch. "What time is it? My watch seems to have stopped again."

"Tea time! I'd have thought your internal clock would have told you that. Are you O.K.? You look a bit green." He reached out a hand to help her down and immediately snatched it away again. "Hey! Your batteries are overcharging – you gave me an electric shock! And look at your hair – it's flying out at right-angles!"

Vaguely she reached up to smooth it down. "I've got pins and needles again, but I didn't think it was contagious!''

"Nor did I." He looked at her consideringly. "You haven't seen any hares prancing around, I suppose?''

"Hares?" she echoed blankly.

"Oh, forget it. I was only joking." He stooped and retrieved her paperbacks from the grass, smoothing their sun-curled pages. "Come on, let's go down. I'm hungry, even if you're not."

He turned and set off across the short scrubby grass. Vanessa paused for a moment to lay the flat of her hand against the Stone in an instinctive gesture of farewell. Then, slightly embarrassed, she ran down the hill after her brother.

It was quite an operation to get Marion settled comfortably in the sitting-room at Conningley, and both Brian and Gavin were sweating freely by the time they had accomplished it. Marion herself, her face drawn with pain, lay back exhausted against the banked cushions and closed her eyes. Julia looked down at her anxiously, wondering whether her insistence on her friend's coming had after all been unwise.

As though reading her mind, Marion's eyes flickered open and she smiled wryly. "Now you see why I'm reluctant to move! It's all right, Julia, don't look so worried. Give me ten minutes to get my breath back and I'll be as right as rain."

Reassured, Julia sat down near the sofa, thankful that she had warned the family to keep out of sight until Marion was settled. She took the glass Gavin handed her, saw that her hand was shaking, and was annoyed that Marion's infirmity should still have this effect on her.

"Not regretting having asked me already, are you?"

Marion's eyes were as mocking as ever and she forced herself to relax.

"Indeed I'm not! In fact I was just indulging in a little self-congratulation at having succeeded in getting you here!

Welcome to Conningley, Marion. Let's hope it's the first of many visits!'"

"If someone will help me, I'll drink to that!"

Julia stood quickly, forestalling Brian's instinctive movement, and held the special cup to her friend's lips.

"Thanks." Marion leaned her head back against the cushions. "I certainly approve of what I've seen of it, anyway. Lucky Brian happened to see the advertisement. Now, where's that family of yours? I'm ready to hold audience!"

The initial awkwardness that Nick and Vanessa experienced was soon completely dissipated by Hilary's complete naturalness and Julia, breathing a sigh of thankfulness, was able to slip away to see to the lunch.

After a few moments Brian followed her through to the kitchen, slipped an arm round her waist and kissed her cheek. "Bless you, Julia. I haven't seen her as relaxed and happy as this for months."

"If we can manage to build up her confidence she might well become altogether more adventurous. Marion's always been a fighter."

"I wish you'd been here all along," he said soberly. "I tried to persuade her to make an effort but she just closed up and I couldn't get through to her at all. Perhaps I used the wrong approach, I don't know."

She glanced up at him. "You look tired, Brian. When did you last have a holiday?"

He shrugged. "I get my annual leave from the office, if that's what you mean."

"And you just spend it at home?"

"Yes. I suppose I could have gone away. Marion tried to persuade me to. She has Daisy and Miss Fergusson to look after her, but – well, to be honest I didn't feel like making the effort. It's not much fun going off on your own, and all our friends are married."

"Gavin still has a week of his holiday left. We'll have to see if we can't fix something. Perhaps you could go off golfing together. I'd be glad to move down with Marion while you're away, if it would make you feel happier about leaving her."

"That's very sweet of you, but let's leave it for now. Just having you all back again is enough for the moment. Aren't the children grown up now? You must be very proud of them. I rather regret not having had a family, but as you know Marion always preferred horses and dogs to babies!"

"You can borrow ours any time!" Julia said with a laugh, deliberately lightening the conversation. "This last term, waiting for Hilary's results and with both O and A levels inflicted on us, was just about as much as we could stand!"

He smiled. "It seems no time since Hilary was bandaging her dolls and Nick flat on his stomach playing trains. Now she's a doctor and he'll doubtless end up chairman of British Rail!"

Julia laughed and lifted the joint back into the oven. "He's switched his allegiance to gliders. Tell me now, what would be the easiest way to serve Marion's meal? Do you think she'd like to eat first, or shall I cut it up so you can help her at table with the least possible fuss?"

"I think she'd prefer to be as much a part of the gathering as possible. Incidentally, she really ought to have a rest after lunch, if that can be arranged. The journey and the excitement will have tired her."

"No problem. Would you ask the girls to come and help me carry things through? It's ready now."

The meal was a great success, with quite a festive air about it. Hilary, who, during her student days, had developed the habit of eating twice as quickly as anyone else, took over Marion's feeding halfway through the meal.

"I'll do it now, Uncle. Your lunch is getting cold."

"Thanks." He smiled up at her as she came round to take his place next to Marion. "But a little less of the 'Uncle', young lady! Surely you can all drop that now – it makes me feel about ninety!"

"I can't!" Vanessa said decidedly, amid the general laughter. "You'll always be Uncle Bran and Auntie Marion to me."

When lunch was over the couch was wheeled back to the sitting-room and the curtains drawn for Marion's sleep. The rest of them settled on the terrace with their coffee, talking desultorily in low voices. Brian was aware of a great feeling of of peace. There was nowhere on earth he would rather have been at that moment than on this sun-dappled terrace with his closest friends.

Fondly his eyes moved over them as he reflected that, although the intervening years had hardly changed Gavin and Julia, they had made a considerable difference to their offspring. Hilary was now a lovely young woman, whose soft mouth and dreamy eyes seemed at variance with that clear, scientific brain, while Nick, with bony wrists and ankles, was still at the gawky stage. And Van. His eyes softened. Dear little Van, who stubbornly insisted on calling him Uncle still. She at least, despite the small, tender swellings under her T-shirt, was still a child and he thanked God for it. She caught his eye and smiled across at him.

"Would you like to come for a walk, Uncle Bran?"

"Oh Vanessa!" Gavin groaned. "Can't you just relax for a while?"

But Brian, seeing the disappointment on her face, rose to his feet. "All right, honey, I'll come for a walk with you. If I don't make a move soon I shall go to sleep! Where would you like to go?"

"I'll give you three guesses!" Nick muttered under his breath. Brian glanced at him interrogatively and he added, "Van's got a thing about that old Stone up there."

"Up where? On the hill?"

Vanessa's face had flushed. "I thought you might like to see it," she said defensively.

"Why not? Come on then, let's go."

With a defiant look at her brother, Vanessa led the way

up the slope of the grass, Brian at her side. No-one else showed any inclination to join them.

"Can you get on to the hill from the garden, then?"

"Yes, there's a gate at the top." She shot him a glance under her thick lashes. "There's a legend that the Stone comes to drink at our well on Midsummer Day and the gate was put in so it could still get there after the house was built."

"You've a well in the garden?"

She nodded. "It's very old, too. Adam Sandys says it was excavated a few years ago and they found Bronze Age pottery and a skull two thousand years old. There it is."

They emerged into the clearing and Brian looked at the dank grey stone with distaste. "Well, I'm sure it's all very fascinating, but give me running hot and cold any day!"

"Oh Uncle, don't *you* be like that! Mummy and the others made rude remarks about it, but I thought you'd understand."

He looked at her quickly, cursing himself for not gauging her mood correctly and aware of having let her down. "I'm sorry, Van. Tell me about it. How old is it, exactly?"

"It could be as much as five thousand years. Doesn't it give you a funny feeling, to think of how the world was when it was built, and of all that has happened since, and it's still here?"

"That's quite a thought, isn't it? It must have been here long before the Romans, then."

"Oh yes. Perhaps even before the Celts, though they would have used it. Adam says it was probably they who threw in the head — to give the water special powers."

Brian looked curiously at her wrapt face. "You seem to know a lot about it. Still, it was a stone we set out to see, wasn't it?"

"Yes, and that's even more interesting."

Brian stifled a sigh. If he was supposed to go into transports of delight at the sight of decaying ancient monuments, he would probably have done better to have stayed on the terrace after all. But Vanessa, unaware of his misgivings, had opened the gate invitingly, and, as he stepped through it, slipped her hand happily in his.

"You'll love the Stone," she said confidently. "It's so old and wise and yet so welcoming."

What an imagination the child had! he thought with amusement. But as they came up over the crest of the hill and he had his first sight of the Druid Stone a strong tremor shook his body and he stopped abruptly. Vanessa looked at him in surprise.

"What's the matter?"

"Nothing." He found it hard to speak. All at once he felt cold and wretchedly sick. Far from kindly, the megalith that loomed up before them struck him as evil and menacing and he had the most absurd impulse to turn and run.

"Uncle!" Vanessa was shaking his hand. "What is it? What's wrong?"

He pulled himself together with an effort which brought beads of perspiration to his face. "Sorry. Just – someone walking over my grave, I suppose."

"Come and see the Stone, then."

When he still didn't move she tugged impatiently at his hand, and, because he had no choice, he went stumbling beside her across the rough grass to the lowering, implacable monument that seemed to fill the whole earth and sky.

"Put your hand against it," his tormentor insisted. "There! Can you feel the tingle?"

He nodded dumbly, unable for a moment to remove his hand which remained clamped against the Stone as wave after wave of pain flowed from it up into his arm. With a jerk he wrenched it away. His face was livid and he was gasping for breath.

"Uncle Bran! Are you sure you're all right?" Vanessa's voice came and went in waves of sound. "Sit down and lean against the Stone for a minute."

"No!" The violence of his reaction startled her. He took out a handkerchief and wiped his face. He could feel sweat pouring down his body in an enervating flood. "I'm sorry, Van. I probably shouldn't have sat in the sun so soon after a big meal."

"I'm sorry, too, but I had to bring you. It wanted to see you."

He stared at her uncomprehendingly. "What did?"

"The Stone."

He said through his teeth, "Then I hope it's satisfied."

She moved away from him and he watched her as she spread-eagled herself against the monument, head back, eyes closed in a kind of ecstasy.

"It recharges me," she said softly. "Any time I'm tired or fed-up I only have to come here and lean against the Stone and the tingles fill me with – with power and excitement."

She stopped and a tremor crossed her face. She said questioningly, "Bran?"

"Yes?"

"Bran!" There was a queer, ringing note of exultation in her voice that sent a superstitious shudder racing down his spine.

"Vanessa!" he said sharply. "It's time to go back."

Slowly her eyes opened, focusing on him with difficulty. "Why, what time is it? My watch has stopped."

"How do you know it has? You haven't looked at it."

"It always does, when I'm up here. Perhaps it's the vibrations. Or perhaps," she added, smiling slightly, "being designed to record time, it's useless when it comes in contact with timelessness!"

He moistened his lips. "Well, to answer your question it's nearly four. Marion will have woken up by now and I think we should go back."

"All right. Are you feeling better?"

"Yes, thank you." The prospect of leaving the Stone was enough to ensure his recovery. She fell into step beside him and together they went back through the gate and along the path to the lawn. Brian had the absurd impression that everything would have changed, grown immeasurably older in their absence, as though they had visited some alien fairyland where every minute spent was a century of earthly time. But everything seemed just as they'd left it.

Gavin looked up from his paper as they came down the grass. "Julia's just gone in to Marion. Had a good walk?"

Vanessa merely nodded and went into the house. Brian sat down in the chair he'd vacated earlier and sat staring at his clasped hands.

"Have you ever been up there?" he asked abruptly.

"On the hill? No, I haven't yet. I believe the Stone's quite impressive. It's mentioned in all the guide-books."

"It's diabolical!" Brian said explosively.

Gavin looked at him in surprise. "How do you mean?"

"It – gives off the most incredible emanations."

"What the hell are you talking about?"

Brian drew a deep breath "There's some – current running through it. You can feel the vibrations. It put the fear of God into me, I don't mind telling you."

Gavin smiled. "Yes, I've heard of that before. Quite a lot of people have reported experiencing something similar, particularly at Stonehenge. At certain times of the year, probably due to cosmic influences, some of these old stones seem to become electrically charged. No doubt it's the quartz in them."

"Why quartz?" Brian's breathing was becoming steadier. If it was a known phenomenon, perhaps he wasn't going mad after all.

"It vibrates rapidly when influenced by an electric field. That's why it's widely used in electronic communications equipment."

"I see."

"So I doubt if you'll need an amulet after all!"

Brian smiled. "I don't mind admitting it scared me silly, but Van on the other hand seems to have some natural affinity with the thing. She even spoke of it as though it were alive."

"Vanessa has always personified things. It's on a par with talking to plants, I suppose – and Julia does that!"

There were other facets of Vanessa's behaviour up on the hill that had disturbed Brian, but he could think of no way to describe them and Gavin must already think him a fool for reacting so strongly to the Stone. So he determinedly put the episode out of his mind and rose to his feet.

"I'll go and see how Marion is."

Gavin looked after him thoughtfully. He had not paid much attention when Julia had said Brian seemed under a strain but perhaps she had a point after all. His behaviour just now had been odd to say the least, and could hardly be accounted for by a prickling in his fingers from a standing stone. Gavin resolved to keep a careful eye on him, and if necessary steer him in the direction of medical help.

Slightly reassured by his decision, he got to his feet and went into the house to join the others.

Five

The week slowly passed. Vanessa still paid her daily visit to the Stone but she was careful not to lie down on its slab nor, although the temptation was strong, allow herself any prolonged contact with it. Brian's violent antipathy towards it had disturbed her and a vague uneasiness lingered when she recalled her own apparent loss of consciousness up there.

But despite these reservations, her curiosity about it continued to grow, as did her conviction that no personal harm would come to her through the auspices of the Stone. Her temporary withdrawal from physical contact with it was a pause, a marking time, nothing more. Quite apart from this, the weather was not at the moment conducive to spending long hours on the hillside. The sun had disappeared and a cool breeze chased hovering clouds across the sky. Vanessa resigned herself to helping her mother and sister empty the last packing-cases which the removal men had left and stack them out in the garage to await collection.

The weather continued to deteriorate during the week and Thursday dawned cool and dark with rain. Hilary and Julia had arranged to spend the day shopping in London and they left early with Gavin who was going to drop them at the station. Shortly afterwards Vanessa heard the phone ring and moments later Nick put his head round her door.

"That was a boy I met at the club. He's invited me round for the day. Tell Mum we'll probably be going to the flicks so I may not be in for dinner."

"All right."

Rather disconsolately she watched from her bedroom window as, encumbered by his yellow cape, he cycled down the drive, circled the green, and turned on to the main road. The green itself was smothered by an oppressive blanket of rain. A few ducks came out of the pond and straddled, preening their feathers, on the wet grass. The giant chestnut stood gloomily weighted down by its mass of foliage, the bench which encircled its trunk dark with rain. On the far side of the main road the roofs of the bungalows gleamed wetly and beyond them the fields were shrouded in mist.

Vanessa sighed and turned away, kicked off her shoes and curled up on the bed with her Agatha Christie. But the repetitive drone of the vacuum cleaner impinged on her concentration, as did awareness of the appoaching presence of the woman who pushed it. Soon she would reach this room and move methodically round it, while her pale, animal-eyes kept darting in her direction.

Vanessa shuddered and sat up. If only there was

somewhere she could go out of Mrs Hare's reach! And like the answer to her wish she remembered the small privacy of the summer-house, never visited since that first day of arrival.

Moving at last with a sense of purpose, she put on an extra sweater, collected an old travelling-rug and stuffed some apples and a bar of chocolate into the pockets of her mac. Then, having listened to ensure that Mrs Hare was still upstairs, she crept into the kitchen and lifted off the hook the long, rusty key which hung below the spare one to the garage.

Minutes later she was removing her dripping mac and hanging it on a convenient nail. It was damp and rather cool in the summer-house and she was glad of the extra sweater. She laid her book on the sloping surface of the old table and looked about her. Apart from the elderly deck-chair there was no other furniture in the little room. Ancient cobwebs festooned the corners and generations of spiders lay withered and dry on the window-sills. A shelf ran round the wall about shoulder-height and Vanessa moved along it hopefully but it contained little of interest: a collection of lidless jam jars, an old stained painting of a rose garden in a broken frame, an ancient pair of gardening gloves. Not exactly a treasure trove, she thought ruefully, but then one didn't expect treasure on open shelves. If there was anything of interest here it would be hidden away from casual gaze. Her eyes went up automatically to the dark, dusty corners immediately under the roof space, and excitement quickened inside her. But how to reach them? Neither the table nor the chair would support her weight, but perhaps if she could gain a foothold on the narrow window-sill –

Grasping hold of the old window-frame she pulled herself up, ducking her head to avoid banging it on the low ceiling and, holding on to the frame with one hand, she reached the other into the nearest roof space. There was nothing there, nothing but the thick dusty stickiness of spiders' webs and the dried corpses of dozens of flies.

Grimacing she wiped her hand down her jeans and inched her way along the sill until she could repeat her exploration in the other corner. Again she was disappointed. Her fingers dislodged a small piece of wood which fell with a clatter and its removal revealed a nest of woodlice which, grey and gleaming, spilled out of the cavity, making her withdraw her hand quickly. Dispirited, she jumped down to the floor and hesitated, wondering if it was worth repeating her manoeuvre on the other side of the room. Still, it would only take a moment, and once she was satisfied there was nothing to find she could settle in the old deck-chair with her neglected book.

Once more she hauled herself up and stretched out a tentative hand, but this time, with a stab of excitement, her searching fingers closed round something. With held breath she drew out a small, mildewed book and flicked it open. It appeared to be a diary and quite an old one. The leather binding was blotched with damp and the once shiny clasp hung loose and tarnished. Vanessa stuffed it into her pocket and felt again, and again she was lucky, pulling out from its hiding-place a small drawstring bag, damp and faded with age. And there was something inside it, something that rattled as she lifted the bag.

She jumped down and quickly set up the sagging deck-chair. Then, wrapping herself in the travelling-rug for warmth, she sat down to examine her finds.

The cords of the bag, originally of blue silk, had knotted damply together and it took several minutes' impatient tugging before the mouth gaped open and she tipped it upside down over the rug. Five small white pebbles fell out and Vanessa stared down at them curiously, wondering why someone had thought them important enough to conceal so carefully. One of them was larger and flatter than the others, with a hole through which a narrow leather band had been threaded. She picked it up to examine it more closely, and at once the familiar tingle ran through her fingers. So it had some connection with the Druid Stone. Slowly she turned it. There seemed to be a design engraved on one side but it was highly stylized and she couldn't make out what it represented.

The other four pebbles were less interesting. They varied slightly in shape and size but they were all smooth and rolled easily between the fingers. Perhaps the diary would offer some explanation of them.

Hopefully she opened the book, holding it so that such light as could penetrate the grimy windows fell directly on the yellowing pages and the faded, elaborate writing with which they were filled. On the flyleaf was written, with many curls and flourishes, *Clarissa Henry. Her Book*. The first page was dated 1st September 1880. Almost a hundred years ago! Vanessa thought incredulously. It was, however, immediately obvious that the writing would not be easy to decipher. It was very small, with frequent abbreviations and in some places the dampness of the hiding-place had paled it almost to illegibility. And as she turned the pages she saw that the writing became more and more distorted, as though the writer grew increasingly agitated. With a frustrated sigh she turned back to the first page and began to read slowly.

'This Book has been given to me on my nineteenth birthday and I am making haste to start it at once, even though the year is far spent, for the purpose of recording the strange occurrences which have befallen me since the start of this summer. Sometimes I fear I may be losing my reason, and perchance recording them here may allow some recognizable pattern to emerge from all the strangeness. It all relates, of course, to the Stone which stands on the hilltop above our House.'

Vanessa came to an abrupt halt, her finger marking the place she had reached. She was suddenly very hot and she fumbled with one hand to free herself from the restricting folds of the rug. Then, greedy for more information, her eyes went back to the page in front of her.

'There is a strange woman in the village who tells stories concerning the Stone, and Lettice and I have laughed over them together in the winter evenings. But, since the hot weather came, I have become unwilling to dismiss them so cursorily. For it seems – and it is here that I begin to doubt my sanity – that there may indeed be truth in them. Firstly, she vows the Stone has powers – that it is capable of movement and comes to drink from the well in our garden on certain nights of the year. Also, and this is indeed gruesome, having some link, I believe, with pagan times, she swears that every hundred years or so it still exacts a sacrifice – which must needs take the form of a severed human head.'

Again Vanessa stopped, lifting her eyes from the cramped, difficult letters which fled higgledy-piggledy over each other across the yellowing pages. A severed head – the skull in the well – the *tête coupée* Adam had spoken of as one of the most widespread Celtic practices.

An extra large raindrop pattered against the glass behind her like the tap of a ghostly hand and she started violently, heart racing. Perhaps after all this dark, damp seclusion was not the best place to read through the diary. In any case she really needed help in deciphering it, preferably from someone familiar with old-fashioned writing, who would understand the frequent and mystifying abbreviations.

Adam Sandys – of course! His work must involve him in reading many such manuscripts and in addition he knew not only about the ancient cult of the head but also legends concerning the Stone itself.

Disentangling herself from the last folds of the rug, Vanessa hurriedly dropped the pebbles back into the bag and pulled the cord tight. Then she pushed it and the diary deep into her mac pocket and shrugged on the still-wet garment. The rug and paperback she could collect later. Now it was imperative to seek out Adam Sandys.

With head down against the rain she pushed her way

back through the branches that overgrew the little path and, skirting the house, hurried down the drive to the front gate. Only as she came abreast of the green did she ease her pace slightly. On her right the little pub garden where they had eaten their lunch on moving day was bleak and deserted, its green metal tables collecting pools of water, its gaily-coloured umbrellas closed and dripping with rain. A car sped along the main road and she was glad to see it. That summer of a hundred years ago had gained too firm a hold on her mind and she was thankful to escape from it to the safety of today. Yet was this summer any safer? The Stone still had its mysterious powers, as none knew better than herself.

She crossed the road and hurried past the shops where last week she had looked for employment, counting them off in her head until she should reach the diamond-paned bowfront of *Sandys of Time*. And here it was.

With a sigh of relief she pushed open the door and cannoned straight into Adam Sandys himself. He was standing just inside the doorway talking to a tall, attractive girl who was engaged in fastening a waterproof cape round her shoulders.

"Good morning," he said politely, cutting short her apologies. "Can I – oh, it's Vanessa, isn't it? Hello!"

"Hello," she answered shyly, wishing the tall girl would take her leave.

"What can I do for you? Are you here on behalf of your mother?"

"No, I –" Despite herself, she glanced again at the girl beside her.

"I'm sorry. This is Louise Dunne, a friend of mine. Louise – Vanessa Prior, whose family has come to live at Conningley."

Louise nodded and murmured a conventional greeting, her interest suddenly aroused. This, then, must be the younger sister of the girl who had claimed Adam's attention last Friday. He was waiting patiently for her to explain her requirements, and eventually she said hesitantly,

"I – rather wanted a word with you, if it's convenient."

"I'm sorry, Vanessa, I'm afraid it isn't just at the moment. I've promised to run Louise back to Aylesbury. Can Miss Bingley help?" He nodded towards a grey-haired woman who stood discreetly behind a counter further down the shop.

Vanessa battled to hold down her disappointment. "No, not really. That is – I'd rather speak to you."

"Unfortunately I'll be in Aylesbury for the rest of today, and tomorrow I have to go to Amersham. I could manage Saturday, if that's any good?"

Saturday! She needed to speak to him now – at once!

"I suppose so," she muttered ungraciously.

"It's nothing urgent, is it?"

"Not really, I suppose. I just wanted to show you something I'd found."

"Right, well if you're sure Miss Bingley can't help we'll make it Saturday, shall we?"

He held open the door with a smile, and because she had no option she went through it, followed by Louise who waited by the little red sports car for Adam to open it. Disconsolately, Vanessa turned towards home.

"That you, Miss?" Mrs Hare appeared at the kitchen door as she came into the hall. "I've been looking for you. Your lunch is ready."

"Thanks. I'll – just take my mac upstairs."

She hurried past the woman and ran up to her bedroom. There she extracted the diary and bag of pebbles from her pocket and slipped them under the pillow, rearranging the counterpane neatly. That would do as a temporary hiding-place.

Mrs Hare had laid a single place at the long dining-room table and Vanessa sat down without comment. With anyone else she would automatically have suggested eating together at the more companionable kitchen table, but not with Mrs Hare.

"Ring the bell, Miss, when you're ready for your sweet."

The flat, animal eyes were on her face, eager, probing. Vanessa looked away and nodded. But by the time she'd finished her meal she acknowledged that she could contain her curiosity no longer, that she must speak to someone about the Stone, and the only choice was Mrs Hare. Slowly she folded her napkin, pushed her chair under the table and went through to the kitchen.

Mrs Hare was standing expectantly in the middle of the room, her hands clasped under her apron.

"Yes, Miss?"

Her voice was taut with excitement. She knows why I've come, Vanessa thought resentfully, casting about for some means of opening the conversation.

"You were here with the people before us, weren't you?" she began abruptly.

"That's right, Miss, I was."

"They weren't here long, were they?"

The woman's nose quivered and Vanessa held back a smile. It was as well Nick wasn't here to catch her eye. "No indeed, Miss. It was six months almost to the day."

Vanessa moistened her lips. "And – why didn't they stay?"

Mrs Hare smiled. "They left, Miss, because their dog wasn't happy! Leastways, that's what they told me. Have you ever heard the like?"

"Their *dog*?"

"Yes, Miss. I must say the creature spent most of its time howling, enough to get on anyone's nerves. But it seems to me it would be easier to get rid of the dog than go to all the trouble and expense of moving house again, when it wasn't strictly necessary, as you might say."

"You don't think that was the real reason?" Vanessa persisted unwillingly.

"Well, yes and no. To my mind it wasn't so much that the animal was unhappy, as *why* it was unhappy, if you get my meaning. I mean, dogs don't usually go about looking as though they were expecting to be beaten, do they, and Mrs Denton swore it had been all right in their last house. A perky, friendly little thing it had been then, she told me. But it had to be positively pushed out in the garden to do its business, and higher than the top of the lawn it just would not go, even when its master and mistress were with it."

"The well frightened it?" Vanessa prompted.

Mrs Hare let out her breath in a long sigh, realizing that the necessary preliminaries had been completed. "The well – and the Stone," she answered quietly.

"But the Stone's nowhere near the garden!"

"Sometimes its Guardian comes down."

Vanessa felt the hairs lift on the nape of her neck. "Its –?"

"It has a Guardian, Miss. One of them elementals it is, a creature, half-man, half-beast. I've seen it myself."

"What does it look like?" Vanessa asked faintly.

"Well now, it's small and dark, and covered with a mat of coarse hair. Enough to give any animal hysterics if it caught sight of it, that I must admit."

"And it – comes here?"

"Sometimes. But there's no need to be frightened, Miss. It would never hurt *you*."

"But why does it come?"

"The last time was because I was late taking up the milk. I'd had a lot to do earlier and it just slipped my mind." Seeing the girl's total incomprehension, she added softly, "The Stone gets thirsty, Miss. I take milk up there every evening and pour it into that little dip in the surface. Of course –" she shot her a sideways glance "– it prefers blood, but that isn't always easy to come by."

Vanessa blindly put out a hand and gripped the back of a kitchen chair. That line of conversation was obviously too dangerous to pursue and she returned to the marginally safer one of her predecessors.

"Did you tell the Dentons about the Guardian?"

"Lord love you, no, Miss. Wasn't no call to."

"Then – why are you telling me?"

"Well, you asked, like," Mrs Hare replied reasonably. "And in any case you'd have found out about it soon enough, being the Priestess. We'll all be working together in the end."

Vanessa said wildly, "I don't know what you're talking about!"

"No, Miss. Never mind, then."

"You're not going to explain?"

"No, Miss. Not right now, anyway. If it frightens you, it still isn't the time for you to know. I wouldn't have said as much as I did if you hadn't asked. Those are my instructions, you see. Answer each question as it's asked but volunteer nothing. I'm sorry if I went too fast for you."

Vanessa wondered dispassionately if she were going to faint again. She had wanted information about the Stone, and most certainly she had been given it. Now she wished uselessly that she had never come to the kitchen, that she had simply retrieved her paperback from the summer-house and spent a safe, happy afternoon in her bedroom with Miss Marple. Even more violently did she wish she had not gone to the summer-house in the first place and taken so much trouble to dig out its hidden secrets. Without the diary, and the pebbles whose significance she had yet to learn, life might have been allowed to continue as it had always done.

Yet dimly she knew that would never have been the case. From the moment her father told Uncle Bran of their proposed return, and he in turn found Conningley for them, the die had been cast and everything else must follow as inevitably as the night did the day.

Mrs Hare must have realized her line of thought and it was she who terminated their conversation. "Well, if you'll excuse me, Miss, I've the dishes to see to."

Vanessa nodded and turned away, stumbling like a somnambulist up the stairs to her bedroom. It was all so puzzling; at times everything seemed crystal-clear in her mind and she understood exactly what it was all about.

Then, when she tried to think back, sometimes only minutes later, the explanations completely eluded her. She did not understand how her memory could suddenly become so selective; she had never noticed it before.

Had she but known it, it was this selectivity, this eradication of memory between one flash of insight and another, which was to prove her greatest blessing and which, in the final analysis, saved her sanity.

Six

"Are you coming home before this dinner of yours this evening?" Julia asked her husband at breakfast the next day.

"Yes. For one thing I'll need to wash and change and for another I want to leave the car here. I've been warned there's a lot of drink flowing on these occasions, so it seemed a sensible precaution to arrange for a car to take us and bring us back. Brian's calling for me at six-thirty and we'll go in together."

"How will he get home afterwards?"

"Presumably the hired car will take him on to Kimble."

"Since his own car will be here he might as well spend the night with us and drive home in the morning. Tomorrow's Saturday, after all."

"Yes, that probably would be best. I'll phone him at the office and suggest it."

"You might also ask him if he and Marion would like to come over again on Sunday. It seemed a great success last week and I haven't had a chance to go down and see her since. Incidentally, I've been meaning to warn you not to mention the Pembrooks' party to Brian."

"Oh Lord yes, that's next weekend, isn't it? Why shouldn't I mention it?"

"It's just that Brian and Marion used to be very friendly with that crowd and I rather gather there hasn't been much contact since the accident."

"We don't have to go, do we?" Nick asked apprehensively. "To the Pembrooks'?"

"It was an open invitation. The three of you would be very welcome, but if you've 'something better to do', as Linda put it, they'll quite understand. The twins will be there, of course, and quite a few other young people. Wouldn't you like to see them again?"

"In a word, no! It was bad enough having to go to all those ghastly tea-parties when we were little. The twins were the wettest of the lot!"

"Remember that they're now young ladies of seventeen and might be a lot more interesting!"

Nick merely grunted and Vanessa said mischievously, "This might be your chance, Nick. You were complaining to Steve about the shortage of girls in Ickfield!"

Nick coloured. "You little brat! Were you eavesdropping?"

"Of course not but you were on the phone as I came downstairs and I couldn't help hearing that bit."

"I'm a darn sight more interested in gliding anyway," Nick affirmed doggedly. "Which reminds me, Dad. You know I mentioned before I'd like to learn? Well, Steve was saying yesterday you can join as a day member, just to try it out and see if you like it. Would it be all right if I had a go this afternoon?"

"I suppose so, if you've enough money!"

"Thanks – that'll be great!"

"It's quite an expensive hobby, I imagine, so don't get carried away – either literally or metaphorically!" Gavin stood up and bent to kiss his wife. "See you later, then. Have a good day. At least the weather seems to be improving at last."

"Do you realize," Julia remarked, setting down her coffee cup, "that we have now been in the house two whole weeks? In some ways it seems more like two years!"

"And it's a week since I came back from Italy," Hilary added. "That seems another lifetime, too."

The same thought was with Adam Sandys that morning as he drove along the road to Amersham. On his last trip he hadn't had the car, and that had led to his meeting with Hilary Prior. A week ago, and he hadn't seen her since. It was slightly disconcerting that, despite that, he found himself continually thinking about her. Louise had been quick to notice his preoccupation and she'd returned to her questioning yesterday, after Vanessa had called at the shop. He wondered again what it was that she'd wanted. A pity he hadn't been able to stop to talk to her, but Louise had been anxious to get back to the office with the manuscript he'd vetted for her. However, he told himself with a faint smile, at least it gave him an excuse to call at the house the next day. He thought again of the little hedged path leading to the well and hoped he hadn't scared them with all his talk of the skull and bones that had been found there. It was not the kind of association everyone relished for their back garden!

Brian put down the phone and sat for a moment tapping his pen on his desk. He was looking forward to the evening with Gavin; it was a long time since he'd spent one in all-male company. In fact, he frequently felt an outsider nowadays in his own home, full of women as it was. Since Marion's accident, the whole focus of the house had shifted to the room where she lay which, to his shame, he had come to loathe. Yet if he tried to relax with books and records in the pleasant sitting-room downstairs, he was sooner or later overcome by a sense of guilt which inevitably led to his going up to join her, even though he sometimes suspected that his company caused her more irritation than pleasure.

Perhaps life really would be easier, now that the Priors

were back. There was Sunday to look forward to as well; Gavin had mentioned on the phone that they were welcome to go over again, and Marion had been noticeably less difficult since last week's visit. However, he thought on a wave of discomfort, this time he would certainly not be cajoled into visiting that infernal Stone. He frowned slightly, wondering, from the distance of five days, exactly what about it had upset him so much. Remembered fear, like remembered pain, retains nothing of its potency and it now seemed ludicrous that he should have gone so far as to admit his phobia to Gavin.

A tap on the door recalled him from his introspection and, dismissing his private life from his thoughts, he accepted the stack of letters which his secretary handed him.

Vanessa had been restless all day. During the morning, secure in her room and with the comforting awareness of her family around her, she had opened the diary again and flicked quickly through it searching for some clue to the presence of the pebbles. Eventually, just before lunch, she did come across a reference to them.

'... she pressed into my hand several small, round stones, closing my fingers about them when I would have dropped them in consternation at the sensation they produced on my skin, a most unpleasant prickling which almost painful. One of them, she informed me in a hoarse whisper, had a hole right through the centre. I was to thread it on a ribbon and wear it about my neck, when all would become clear to me! A fancy tale indeed! Does she take me for an ignorant village wench who indulges in such rituals in the hope of seeing her lover's face?

'I would have handed back the stones at once, but no sooner had she instructed me than she turned and hurried away. I declare I am becoming increasingly vexed with Mistress Hare and her importunities.'

Mistress Hare? Vanessa's head snapped up. But that

wasn't possible, surely? As logic reasserted itself she gave a shaky little laugh. Not the *same* Mrs Hare, stupid! Yet it was odd that all those years ago *a* Mrs Hare should have been connected with the Stone. Perhaps the family had assumed permanent care of it, daughter taking over from mother as she had read that witches did.

She tipped the pebbles out of the bag and rolled them round the palm of her hand, accepting without flinching the painful tingling which, a hundred years ago, had disconcerted Clarissa Henry. Then, letting the others slide on to the bed, she lifted the stone with the hole, holding each end of its thong and letting it swing like a pendulum. For a while she gazed at it intently, then, with a little sigh, dropped it on to the bed with the others. It was not quite time to wear it yet. Later, she would slip it round her neck, and 'all would become clear'.

The golf club dinner was a great success. Brian knew several of the men present and Gavin had introduced him to others from his firm. They established an instant camaraderie which added greatly to the enjoyment of the evening and strengthened in Brian a resolution to join the club himself. He was, after all, entitled to some relaxation away from the strangling grip of the house he still thought of as home.

He realized he was drinking considerably more than usual and blessed Gavin for his foresight in securing the services of a driver for the journey home. The food was excellent, the speeches brief and witty and the entertainer, a comedian well-known from his television appearances, provided just the right note of *risqué* humour to appeal to his audience in their present state of well-being.

"I don't know when I've enjoyed myself so much," Brian remarked as he settled himself next to Gavin on the comfortable back seat of the hired car. "It was very good of you to invite me."

"Not at all. I'm delighted you could come. Do you good

to cut loose occasionally. If you don't mind my saying so, old man, you do sometimes strike me as being a mite too — well, self-contained."

"Needs must, wouldn't you say?"

Gavin reddened. "Sorry if I'm speaking out of turn. Put it down to the booze!" And yet, he thought privately, though he had spoken without thinking, it had been from his long acquaintance with Brian that he'd formed that opinion, not from the few occasions on which he'd seen him since their return to Buckinghamshire. Truth to tell, Brian had always struck him as rather a cold fish and perhaps, poor devil, as things turned out it was just as well.

For one maudlin, soul-searching moment, Gavin tried to imagine his own reaction had it been Julia who was paralysed, and immediately shied away from the idea in something approaching panic. God, who was he to offer criticism? In a fit of contrition he patted his friend's knee.

"Never mind, old man, we'll have us lots more evenings like this, won't we now?"

They lapsed into comfortable silence, and both of them were more than half asleep by the time the car stopped at Conningley. The hall light shone out in welcome, though Julia would have gone to bed long since. Gavin paid off the driver and together he and Brian went into the quiet house.

"One for the stairs?" he offered hospitably.

"Not for me. One more and I mightn't make the stairs!"

"You know where your room is, don't you?"

"Yes, thanks. I took the case up earlier."

"Right, well I'll say good-night. I'm just going to the kitchen for some alka seltzer. There's no hurry in the morning; breakfast will be whenever you're ready."

Brian went softly up the stairs. His room was the one directly across the landing. Julia had apologized for its *décor* but he found it pleasant enough, a pale *eau-de-nil* wash over the walls. In any case, he wasn't, he hoped, going to sit up all night looking at the decorations. He didn't feel tired, though. The doze in the car had been sufficient to refresh

him. He undressed, washed and slipped on his pyjamas.
There was a pile of magazines on the table by the bed –
Punch, Reader's Digest, Country Life. He might glance at them
before he put out the light.

He went across to the window and pushed it wide. It was
a dark, clear night with no moon, but a tapestry of stars
spread overhead. The light from the room behind him fell
in a splash on the terrace below and the first few feet of
grass. Outside its radius all was black and hidden.

Behind him the door of his bedroom clicked softly and he
turned in surprise, supposing Gavin had forgotten to tell
him something about the morning's arrangements. He was
totally unprepared to see Vanessa who, having closed the
door behind her, was leaning against it and looking across
at him with a faint smile. She was wearing a plain cotton
nightdress and a stone of some sort hung round her neck.

"Van – hello!" he said awkwardly. "What's the matter?
Can't you sleep?"

"Bran!" she said softly, and the first prickle of unease
inched up his scalp. There was in her voice that low,
vibrating note with which she had spoken last Sunday up
by the Stone.

He gave a nervous little laugh. "I think you'd better go
back to bed, young lady. It's not –" He broke off as she
started to move towards him and his discomfort deepened.
For nothing about her other than the basic features of nose,
mouth and hair bore any resemblance to the Vanessa he
knew. Her body moved with a fluid grace he had never seen
before and her eyes were fixed on him with an intensity
from which he was powerless to look away, no longer the
eyes of a fifteen-year-old girl but old beyond his
comprehension – hundreds, thousands of years old, and in
their depths the knowledge of all women through the ages.

She had come right up to him, so close that he was aware
of leaning slightly backwards, the ridge of the window-sill
cutting into his back.

"Bran the Blessed!" she said haltingly, in that low,

throbbing voice. She raised her hands and ran them lightly over his face, fingers caressing nose, lips and beard and moving up over his ears and hair until gooseflesh rippled over him. He caught hold of her wrists and pulled her hands down.

"Now look, Van, I don't know what this is all about, but that's quite enough." He could hear the bluster in his voice. "Whatever would –"

She moved before he was ready for her, while his hands still circled her wrists and were powerless to push her away. Rising suddenly on her toes she pressed her mouth hard against his. There was one frozen second of shocked disbelief, followed immediately by a white-hot flame which shot through his body like a blade. With the ruthlessness of sudden fear he wrenched himself free of her, holding her away from him with all the strength his shaking arms could muster.

"What the hell are you playing at? Are you mad? Get out of here at once, or I'll call your father!" He was too distraught to appreciate the ridicule inherent in a situation which required Gavin to protect him from Vanessa. "Go on, now!"

He gave her a little push but she evaded his hand and came close again, her body moving sinuously against his, fingers reaching up again to his face. He dug his fingers viciously into the soft flesh of her arms and marched her to the door, the blood drumming in his temples and a red haze before his eyes.

"Out!" he said thickly. "And don't you ever try those tricks on me again!"

She turned her head and he stared for a moment longer into the familiar, unknown face. Then she smiled, a drugged, uncomprehending little smile, and she was still smiling as he thrust her out on to the landing and pressed the door shut. There was no key in the lock, he noticed agitatedly. God help him if she came back later.

Clumsily he moved over to the dressing-table and leaned

on it heavily, head bent. What in heaven's name had got into her? What was she trying to prove? Did she imagine –?

The memory of her mouth on his and her hard, firm little breasts pressing against him swept over him suddenly and the burning shaft lanced him again. He felt the sweat start up, in his armpits, above his lip.

"God!" he said violently, aloud. "It was *Van!*"

After a long time he switched off the light and lay down on top of the bed, his arms behind his head, and for the next hour or so every creak and rattle of the old house brought him to a sitting position, eyes on the door. But it remained closed and gradually he forced himself to relax. Even so, it was one of the most restless nights of his life. Time and again he was brought up sharply by the sheer impossibility of what had happened: Van, who was always so sweet and natural with him, so completely at her ease, who only last week had insisted on still calling him 'Uncle'. She hadn't tonight, though even then it had been the old, baby version of his name she had used. What was it she'd said – 'Bran the Blessed'? What the hell was that supposed to mean? That she –?

His teeth fastened in his lip, blotting out the memory of her. It *couldn't* have happened. Perhaps, he began to think towards morning, it really hadn't but had been a hallucination brought on by the amount he'd had to drink. Yet if he were given to erotic fantasies – which he wasn't – Vanessa was positively the last person in the world about whom he would have them. A child, for God's sake! A child of fifteen! There were names for men who lusted after little girls, and they weren't pleasant. No, God help him, he wouldn't accept that accusation. Never in all his life had he thought of Vanessa or any other young girl in such a light. It was sick – evil.

Yet here in his room she had not seemed a young girl. Not only her behaviour but her whole appearance had been out of character. She had been, quite blatantly, a seductress: Salome, Delilah, Jezebel. There must be modern equivalents but it was those ancient, legendary names that came most readily to mind, seemed most appropriate. And that gliding, ethereal quality; it was almost as though she were drugged.

His eyes snapped open again. Could that be the answer? Could the little fool possibly be experimenting with LSD or something? He'd heard kids did nowadays, even those from loving, stable homes. If that was the answer she was quite liable to throw herself out of a window – anything. Briefly he pondered whether he should go and check that she was asleep but he knew in his heart that he did not dare. Anyway it was hours now since she'd left him. Any effects would surely have worn off and there'd been no sound of any disturbance earlier.

At last sheer exhaustion claimed him, but his brief sleep was tormented by fragmented distortions of dreams, all centred exclusively on Vanessa, so that when he woke again as the first light seeped into the room he was no longer sure exactly what had happened and how much his sleeping imagination had conjured up for him. Of only one thing was he certain: he could not face seeing her at breakfast. At the moment, indeed, he felt as though he never wanted to see her again.

Wearily he climbed out of bed and stretched. The window was still wide open as he'd left it and at the top of the garden the overnight mist was lifting, leaving a silver carpet of dew on the grass. Swiftly he washed and dressed, pushed his night-things into the overnight bag and let himself silently out of the room.

The door just to the left of the stairs stood wide open and he was unable to stop himself glancing inside. Vanessa lay with her hands on the pillow on either side of her head like a sleeping child. Her hair was spread over the pillow and her lips slightly parted. For a long moment, aware of the turmoil inside him, he stood and stared at her. Then he went on down the stairs. In the kitchen he found a message pad on the wall. On it he wrote: 'Woke early and was seized with an irresistible urge to rush home and cut the grass! Thanks for your hospitality. Sorry, but we can't make Sunday after all.'

He left it propped up on the kitchen table and let himself quietly out of the still-sleeping house. If he hadn't gone to the dinner – if he'd taken the hired car on to Kimble – what then?

Viciously he stuck the key in the ignition and despite its night outdoors the car started instantly. Slowly and carefully he drove over the gravel to the gate and out into the fresh bright morning.

Seven

It was Hilary who opened the door. She was wearing a T-shirt and shorts and her long legs were golden from the Italian sun. His pleasure at seeing her was even stronger than he'd expected, especially when her face lit up in welcome.

"Hello!" she said. "Come in. What can we do for you?"

"I've come to see your sister, as arranged."

"Vanessa?" She looked at him a little blankly.

"She called at the shop the other day. Didn't she tell you?"

"No. No, she didn't." She pushed open a door on their left. "If you'd like to wait here for a moment I'll go and find her."

Damn! He stood helplessly in the middle of the long room, aware of having mishandled the situation. She had seemed pleased to see him, had perhaps supposed that he'd come to see her, and without even enquiring how she was he'd immediately asked for Vanessa.

His self-reproaches were interrupted by Vanessa herself. She looked rather pale, especially after Hilary's golden glow, and there were large purple bruises at the top of both her arms. He smiled at her.

"Here I am as promised – at your service!" He saw that she was holding a book and a small linen bag.

"Let's go to the summer-house," she said. "We can't really talk here."

"Just as you like."

He followed her through the french windows and up to the top of the lawn, where instead of taking the path he remembered she turned to the right. A moment later they came upon the summer-house, small, slightly dilapidated, with its door standing open and the evocative smell of sun-warmed creosote which always took him back to childhood. Vanessa sat down on the steps in front of it and he joined her.

"Are those what you wanted to show me?" He nodded towards the book and bag on her lap.

"Yes, but first, if you don't mind there are one or two things I'd like to ask you."

"Fire away, then."

"I was wondering if you know anything about the people who used to live here? A long time ago, I mean."

"Not a great deal, I'm afraid. The house was built by Lord Dracombe about the end of the eighteenth century – for a favourite mistress, so the story goes."

"Is there any way of finding out who has lived here since?"

"I imagine it would be in the parish records, Why?"

She looked down at the book on her lap, her hand stroking it thoughtfully. "I found this in the summer-house, wedged into a space under the roof."

"May I see?" He took it from her and opened the flyleaf. "Good lord, Vanessa, this is a find! Whatever made you think of looking up there?"

"I don't know. I just – felt there was something there

somewhere."

"Have you read it?"

"Some of it, but that's why I wanted to see you. It's very difficult to make out with all those scrolls and squiggles and in parts it's badly faded. Then she keeps using abbreviations which I can't understand."

"You want me to transcribe it for you?"

She looked doubtful. "Would it be expensive?"

He laughed. "I shouldn't charge you for it. I'd be only too happy to do it for my own interest. Does it give much insight into their everyday life?"

"No," Vanessa said slowly. "In fact, it's not really written as a diary at all. It – seems to be mainly about the Stone."

He turned to look at her. "The Druid Stone? What about it?"

"Oh – legends and so on." She paused, then handed him the linen bag. "I found these with it."

Curiously he opened the neck of the bag and the pebbles fell into his hand. For a moment he stared at them incredulously, excitement mounting inside him. Then he gave a low whistle and turned them over to examine them more closely.

"This is fantastic – I can hardly believe it! If I'm not mistaken, these are the missing Druid Spell-Stones. They belong in that saucer-shaped hollow in the big Stone, but they disappeared many years ago and no-one could ever find out what had happened to them."

Vanessa was watching him intently. "What were they used for?"

"Oh, all kinds of things! For instance, if a woman wanted to have a child she'd borrow them, or if anyone was ill, or the crops seemed to be failing, but they were always returned to the Stone after use."

He picked up the large, flattish stone with the hole through it. "The tolmaen was especially useful. It could be worn round the neck, or hung in cowsheds to stop witches stealing the milk, or over stable doorways to protect the horses from being hag-ridden. You see the hare engraved on it? It's difficult to make out, but here are the ears, laid along its back, and the legs all bunched together in a leap. The Celts often decorated stones and pieces of metal with animal shapes, and hares were sacred to them.''

He looked up at her, his eyes bright with excitement. "It really is an incredible piece of luck, finding them like this! They ought to be catalogued now and put in the museum for safety.''

"You said they belonged with the Stone.''

"Well yes, originally, but they haven't been there for years and we don't want to risk having them pinched again. Also, I rather doubt that people would know what to do with them anyway in this sceptical age! May I take them with me and pass them on to someone who really knows about such things?''

"No!'' To his surprise she reached over quickly and took them out of his hand.

"But Vanessa you can't hang on to them yourself! They're of enormous historical interest.''

"I don't want to keep them,'' she said, holding them between her two hands, "but you said anyone coud borrow them, so that's what I'm doing. I need them.''

"But –''

"Just until I get my O-level results!'' she added quickly, and he had the impression that she'd seized on that explanation to cover the real one.

"Well,'' he said reluctantly, "you will take care of them, won't you. You say they were with the diary; are they mentioned in it?''

"Yes. Clarissa says they were given to her by – by a woman in the village.'' She hesitated. "Did you feel anything – on your hands – when you held them just now?''

"How do you mean?''

"Every time I touch them they make my skin tingle, and Clarissa mentions the same thing.''

"Really? I can't say I noticed anything myself."

"Adam, you won't tell anyone about them, will you? Not yet."

"But good heavens, Vanessa, be reasonable! Their reappearance is the biggest thing that's happened in the village for years! You really can't expect me to –"

She said rapidly, "If people know they've been found they'll want to take them away and examine them and they might not let me have them back, because of course they're not really mine. But I *need* them, Adam! Please!"

He stared at her for a moment, rather nonplussed by her urgency. "Look, Vanessa, it was only ancient superstition, you know. I shouldn't like to give you the impression that there's really anything in it."

She gave an odd, strained little smile. "I'll take a chance on that. You can have them in a few weeks, I promise, but – not now. And there's no point in telling anyone about them if you can't produce them, is there? You can take the diary, of course. Won't that do to be going on with?"

He smiled slowly. "Well, all right, if it means so much to you. Of course the diary's very interesting too. Just think, if your family hadn't bought the house, these could have remained hidden for another hundred years! And I should say it was a pretty long shot that you heard about it, all the way up there in Newcastle. Or were you in touch with some local estate agents?"

"No, Uncle Bran found it for us."

"Bran, did you say?"

She smiled. "I've called him that since I was a baby, when I couldn't say 'Brian'. He says it makes him sound like a nose-bag, but the name stuck."

"Did you know that Bran the Blessed was one of the ancient Celtic gods?"

"No, I certainly didn't! I thought I'd made the name up myself. What did he do?"

"He was a son of Llyr – Shakespeare's King Lear, who gave his name to Leicester. His chief claim to fame, though, was his head. When he was dying he made his followers cut it off and it stayed alive and went everywhere with them, advising, prophesying, and so on.''

"How horrible!" Vanessa said softly.

"It's a prime example of the cult of the head, which I mentioned the other day.''

"And did Bran's head live for ever?"

"No, eventually it was buried in London facing the Continent, to ward off invaders. A later legend says King Arthur was jealous of it and quite sure he could defend the country himself, so he dug it up and destroyed it.''

She clasped her hands round her knees. "We keep getting back to the Celts, don't we? Tell me more about them. Did they have other sacred animals as well as the hare?"

"Yes, quite a lot – bulls, boars, cats and so on, not to mention a selection of birds. Numbers were very important to them, too, especially three and seven. Remember the old fairy stories, 'seventh son of a seventh son'? It probably all harks back to Celtic mythology.''

"Three's my lucky number," Vanessa said.

He laughed. "I imagine half the people in the country would say the same thing, though they couldn't tell you why. It's amazing how deep-rooted these ancient superstitions are.''

"I chose it because I'm the third child in the family.''

"Well, that might be considered a claim of a sort. When's your birthday?"

"The third of September.''

"Ah-ha! Additional support! The third of the ninth month, being a multiple of three. Let's try your name. Have you a middle one?"

"No, none of us have.''

"Vanessa Prior, then. Twelve letters. Add the two digits together and what do we get? Three again! Right, Vanessa, you've convinced me! I'd say you've more claim than most of us to the number three. Who knows what powers it might have bestowed on you?"

He glanced at her smilingly but her face was wrapt, inward-looking, and he wondered a little anxiously if, despite her interest, he had given her rather a surfeit of blood and superstition for one afternoon. To change the subject, he said the first thing that came into his head.

"Your sister's engaged, isn't she?"

Vanessa turned to him, trying to adjust to a new train of thought. "Yes. Why?"

"Is her fiancé up in Newcastle?"

"No, he's abroad, working in Africa for a year."

"Doing what?"

"Studying tropical diseases. He's a doctor, too."

"Too?"

"Like Hilary."

He turned to stare at her. "Hilary's a doctor?"

"Well, almost. She's passed her finals and now she's going to Rokeby Hospital as a house officer."

"Ye gods!"

Vanessa smiled. "What did you think she did?"

"I hadn't really thought about it. She looks like an actress or a model or something. But a doctor!"

"She's very clever," Vanessa said complacently.

"Yes, she must be." He paused. "How long has she been engaged?"

"Since Easter."

"So he's not been gone long?"

"No, he went out there in April."

Adam was silent. Beautiful, dreamy-eyed Hilary, a doctor! There were more questions he wanted to ask, but it seemed wiser to refrain. Perhaps there'd be a chance of seeing her when they went back to the house. He felt obscurely that he owed her an apology. He glanced again at Vanessa, who'd lapsed back into her own thoughts, rolling the pebbles gently about in the palm of her hand.

"Well, I suppose I'd better be going. I rather think my father was expecting some help in the garden this afternoon! I'll have a go at the diary for you and see whether I can find out about the Henry family. The name does seem vaguely familiar."

"Thanks." She slipped the stones back into their bag and drew the cords tight. "And thank you for coming."

"It's a pleasure. I don't know when I've had such a fascinating afternoon!"

Hilary heard their voices as they came round the side of the house beneath her bedroom window. It had been a long session, that rendezvous in the summer-house. She bit her lip, remembering her embarrassment on discovering that it was Vanessa Adam had come to see. Yet why she should have imagined otherwise —

Her eyes fell to the photograph on the desk in front of her. If Chris hadn't been leaving almost immediately for Africa, would they have become engaged when they did? She rather doubted it. The sparkle had already gone out of their relationship and it had only been the imminent prospect of a long separation which had made them automatically draw close again. She knew now that it had been a mistake, and judging by Chris's stilted, not very frequent letters, she imagined that he knew it too. Certainly those letters weren't bringing him any closer and it was more of a penance than a joy to have to sit down, as she had just done, and answer them. They had outgrown each other, she thought sadly, and this year apart would have brought a natural end to their association if they had only allowed it to. As it was, things were bound to be more complicated.

Not that any of this, she told herself, licking the edges of the air-letter, had anything to do with Adam Sandys, but nevertheless it was pointless to deny that he attracted her. Though she'd managed fairly successfully not to think about him too much during the last week, the instinctive gladness she had felt on seeing him was proof of that.

She heard the door of the next bedroom open, and went out on to the landing. Vanessa was bending over her bed.

"What was all that about?" she asked curiously.

Vanessa spun round. She seemed to have been slipping something under her pillow – something that Adam had given her? Surely she hadn't developed a crush on him? She looked on the defensive and there was a flush on her face.

"Why did you go to the antique shop?" Hilary persisted.

"I wanted Adam's advice on something I'd found. He was just leaving with his girl-friend so he said he'd call round today."

"And what was it you'd found?" Hilary prompted.

"An old diary, written by someone who used to live here."

"The Dentons, you mean? I hope you didn't read it, Van. And what possible reason could you have for thinking Adam would be interested in it?"

Vanessa smiled slightly. "It wasn't the Dentons. The diary's a hundred years old. Adam's going to copy it out for me because it's hard to read."

In spite of herself, Hilary said, "You were up there a long time."

"I suppose we were. He was telling me all kinds of fascinating stories about the Celts."

Hilary's eyes went to the rumpled counterpane. "So he took the diary away with him?"

Vanessa nodded. She was obviously not going to volunteer anything further and Hilary dismissed it with a mental shrug. After all, she was entitled to her secrets. Instead, she said casually, "What was she like, his girl-friend?"

"Tall, smartly dressed."

"Attractive?"

"Yes, I suppose so. She had her hair in a bun-thing, but she'd a pretty face." She shot a sly glance at her sister. "You two should get together instead of asking me all these questions. Adam wanted to know about you, too – how long you'd been engaged and everything."

Hilary felt the colour come to her face.

"He was shattered to hear you're a doctor!" Vanessa added with a giggle. "He seemed to think you should be either a model or an actress!"

Her sister laughed. "Well, I suppose that might be regarded as a compliment! Let's go down and make a cup of tea. You'd better have a wash first, though. You've got dirty smudges on your arms, no doubt from that filthy summer-house."

Vanessa glanced down. "It's not dirt. They're bruises."

"Bruises? However did you get them up there?"

"Probably when Nick was chasing me yesterday. He seems to forget I'm not one of his rough friends!"

"Then for goodness sake tell him to be more careful in future or he'll finish up by breaking your arm."

"Did you know," Vanessa said suddenly as they went together down the stairs, "that Bran was the name of a Celtic god?"

"I can't say I did. Was that one of Adam's gems of information?"

"Yes. His head stayed alive after he died and went on talking to his followers."

"How perfectly revolting!"

"Bran the Blessed, he was called."

"If you ask me, those Celts were a ghoulish lot. Human sacrifices, severed heads – not really to my taste at all! You'd better not let poor Brian know who you've been calling him after all this time – I doubt if he'd appreciate it! By the way, wasn't he supposed to have stayed for breakfast this morning? It was a bit antisocial, creeping out of the house at dawn like that."

"Perhaps he had a hangover and couldn't face the thought of food."

"Possibly. Anyway, Father seems to think he enjoyed himself last night. Poor man, I imagine he has a pretty ghastly life. Marion always did lead him a dance, and it must be a hundred times worse now."

"Don't you like her – Auntie Marion?"

"I certainly never used to, mainly on Brian's behalf. I remember one time at Haddenham overhearing her going on about him to Mother. I was about your age at the time, and I was shocked. He's such a poppet, he really does deserve better."

Gavin put his head round the door. "Did I hear the clink of cups? Good – I thought so! Bring it to the sitting-room when it's ready, would you? Your mother's just changed her mind about the positions of all the pictures in there, so we're starting again from scratch. Just when I thought it was the one room we'd actually got straight!"

"The kettle's almost boiling," Hilary said as he disappeared again. "I'll take the tray through, if you'll bring the teapot."

Vanessa nodded absently. Her mind was still crammed full of Celtic folklore, of sacred hares and spell-stones and the talking head of Bran. She pictured it, of course, like that of Uncle Bran, with his slightly hollow cheeks and the dark, silky beard. How would you carry round a living head? On a salver, like John the Baptist?

She shuddered back to the realization that the kitchen was full of steam, and hastily poured the water into the teapot. As Adam Sandys had said, it had been a fascinating afternoon.

Eight

Julia pressed the doorbell and after a few moments it was answered, slightly to her surprise, by Miss Fergusson. From the recesses of her memory she recalled that Tuesday had always been Mrs Hanbury's half-day.

"Good afternoon. May I see Mrs Cresswell, please?"

"Of course, Mrs Prior. Good afternoon. We're just a wee bit grumpy today, I'm afraid."

Julia stared at her, realized she was referring to Marion, and gave a rather strained smile. "Then perhaps I can cheer her up."

"Aye." There was not a great deal of confidence in the response.

"Don't bother coming up," Julia added quickly. "I'm sure you've a lot to do down here."

"Very well, Mrs Prior. Thank you."

"Marion?" Julia spoke softly, unsure whether she was awake.

The woman on the bed turned her head. "Hello, Julia. You've not chosen a very good day, I'm afraid."

"I intended to come last week but didn't manage it. Is it bad today?"

"Not particularly. I'm wallowing in self-pity, that's all. I get these days from time to time and old Fanny Mackintosh adds fuel to the fire by treating me as though I were about two years old."

"Poor Marion." Julia pulled up a chair and sat down. "Let me see if I can think of anything interesting to tell you. Hilary and I had a day in London, but otherwise not much has happened other than trying to get the house sorted out. It was a pity you couldn't manage Sunday."

"Sunday? How do you mean?"

"Didn't Brian tell you? We asked him on Friday if you could come over again. He said yes at first and then cancelled it, so I gathered he must have remembered something you'd already arranged."

"Of course," said Marion bitterly, "I was forgetting. That was the day we went to Buckingham Palace." She met Julia's enquiring eyes. "Come on, love, what the hell could we have arranged? You know my visit to you last week was the first time I'd been out and we don't exactly hold open house here."

"Perhaps Brian had something on, then?" Julia murmured awkwardly.

"Not a thing. In fact he was mooching in and out of the room all day, nearly driving me mad. Did he by any chance have too much to drink on Friday evening?"

"I didn't see him, but it's possible. Gavin was certainly extremely mellow and I was very thankful he hadn't driven himself home. We were surprised Brian didn't stay for breakfast, though."

"Yes, I heard him come in soon after six. Couldn't think what the dickens he was up to, but he had some story about not having slept too well and out he went before the dew was even off the grass and proceeded to mow it like a maniac! Can you imagine – at seven o'clock on a Saturday morning! But he certainly never mentioned your inviting us for Sunday."

"Perhaps you're right about the hangover, then. He might simply not have felt up to a day out."

"Actually, he's seemed a bit off-colour ever since. Possibly something he ate disagreed with him. He's not used to rich food these days, since he insists on eating whatever I have, which, of course, is totally unnecessary. Lord, how I wish he'd break out occasionally! This endless patience, this turning the other cheek – it's all very well for a while, but there are times when I long for a really good slanging match. It would clear the air all round. But of course Brian prides himself on his infernal self-control. I just hope he isn't over-estimating it or he might finish by beating up old ladies! Anyway, that's enough about us. Have you played any squash yet?"

"No, I'm hoping to have a game one afternoon, but I've had to stay in most days for a succession of carpenters and plumbers – who usually don't turn up anyway!"

Marion smiled. "The outside world doesn't seem to have changed much! What about Linda and Tracy and the rest of them: have they been in touch?" And as Julia hesitated, she went on: "Don't try to spare my feelings, for goodness sake. I haven't seen one of them since I came out of hospital, but they're under no obligation to come and visit me and I don't lose any sleep over it."

"Actually, Linda did phone, yes."

"And?"

"She's invited us over on Saturday to meet some of the old crowd."

"Lucky you. Give them my salaams."

"You know, I'm sure it's just thoughtlessness –" Julia began.

"My dear, I'd probably have behaved the same way myself. They were very good, you know, while I was in Stoke Mandeville, taking it in turns to pop in. It was when it dawned on them that I wasn't going to get any better that they took fright, and you can hardly blame them. They'd been prepared to do the decent thing and visit me for a week or two, but they didn't want the job for life. And let's face it, sport and parties were all that we had in common. If I was to be a total write-off on both counts, what was the point in keeping in touch?"

She smiled ruefully. "Don't look so distressed, Julia. It was probably mainly my own fault. I don't make friends easily – never have. I speak my mind too freely, which isn't the way to make people like you. You're the only real friend I've ever had, and if I carry on much longer in this vein I shall probably lose you too!" She turned her head away abruptly. "God, I mustn't *cry*! I can't even blow my own bloody nose! Sorry, love, I did warn you it was one of those days. Next time I'll hang a yellow flag out of the window, so if you see it turn round and drive straight back home!" She sniffed determinedly and gave Julia a shaky smile. "O.K., balance restored. Well, I hope you enjoy your Haddenham party. I'll be very interested to hear all their news."

"Come on Sunday, then, and we can tell you all about it."

"If Brian allows me to, I shall be delighted."

"Tell him we've fixed it. He's sure to be better by then."

"There is one thing you could do for me," Marion said slowly. "Have him over for a meal occasionally – without me. It would do him good – and me, too. Nothing special, of course, just pot luck *en famille*. He'd love that. And talking of families, your Hilary is much too pretty for her own good. She'll put her patients' blood-pressures up, I don't doubt! Black lashes and grey-green eyes shouldn't be allowed, especially with blonde hair! Vanessa has them too, of course, but she hasn't learned how to use them yet, bless her! She's young for her age, isn't she? Probably with being the baby of the family. It's most refreshing to see her so natural and unspoiled after all the kids her age I used to see around plastered in lipstick and warpaint!"

Julia smiled. "Yes, I suppose she is a young fifteen. She doesn't bother about her appearance at all but no doubt that'll change when she starts to take an interest in boys. At the moment she's still at the pop-star hero-worship stage, which is somewhat one-sided!"

"Brian adores her, you know. She always was his favourite. I can see him now at Haddenham brushing that long hair of hers before she went to bed. Poor Brian! When we married he was quite happy to agree not to have a family but I'm sure he changed his mind as time went on, especially once we started seeing so much of yours. I'm convinced he secretly regards Vanessa as his surrogate daughter!"

But that was not in fact how Brian was thinking of Vanessa that afternoon. Indeed, he had been trying, unsuccessfully, not to think of her at all, but her face kept flooding into his mind, churning it into a whirlpool of conjecture and disbelief while his memory continually played back those four eventful minutes she had spent in his bedroom.

Yet despite this obsessive replay he was no nearer finding any explanation for her behaviour. She could of course have been sleep-walking, but the initial idea would still have had to be present in her subconscious and even this he could not accept. Admittedly he knew nothing of teen-aged girls and their fantasies. Perhaps they did indulge in secret dreams about older men, but it was still impossible that Vanessa should have regarded himself in such a light – impossible, yet at the same time disturbingly exciting.

And it was this underlying rider which was causing him the greatest anguish. The body he had been so confident of controlling and whose needs he had so grossly underrated had flagrantly betrayed him and as a result he was scorched with self-loathing and contempt. One point only could he produce in mitigation. Though the dreams that had plagued him waking and sleeping since Friday were undeniably of Vanessa, it was not as the tousled fifteen-year-old daughter of his friends that she haunted him but as the ageless seductress who had called to him out of a past older than time.

Wearily he ran his hand over his face and started as his secretary raised her voice. "I said are you all right, Mr Cresswell? You don't look very well."

"Yes – yes, quite all right, thank you."

"It's after four," she went on solicitously. "There's nothing that can't wait till the morning, you know. I'll sign these letters if you'd like to leave early."

He looked up at her plain, kindly face. "I think perhaps I will, then, Miss Blake. To be honest I have rather a headache this afternoon. Thank you."

But once on the pavement outside he paused irresolutely. There was nothing to hurry home for, in all conscience; merely an extra hour of trying to decide whether or not Marion wanted him to sit with her. He might just as well relax for a while over a cup of tea.

He made his way stumblingly along the crowded pavements and was about to turn into a café doorway when a touch on his arm spun him round and he found himself gazing with a kind of glazed panic at Vanessa's smiling face.

"Hello, Uncle – I thought it was you! Have you finished

work already?''

He moistened his lips. "Yes, I – was just going to –" He stopped, searched frantically for an escape clause, was unable to find one, and finished lamely, "to have some tea."

She was looking up at him expectantly like a puppy waiting to be fed. Vanessa's capacity for food and drink was a long-standing joke. Because he had no choice, he added almost inaudibly, "Would you like to join me?"

"Oh yes please! I was just trying to work out if I had enough money for a milk shake!"

His temples were pounding as he led her into the noisy, crowded room but she gave no sign of noticing his agitation. Seated opposite him across the small formica-topped table, she gave her undivided attention to the menu and he was free to watch her, scouring her face for any trace of that other self who in so short a space of time had completely disrupted his life. There was none, and he unflexed his hands as the waitress approached them.

"Have you decided, Vanessa?" He sounded almost jocular, he thought wonderingly.

"Could I have an ice-cream sundae? The one with nuts, bananas and honey, please."

Brian closed his eyes on a wave of nausea. "And a pot of tea for me," he added quietly.

The important task disposed of, Vanessa settled back in her chair and flashed him a smile. "I've been trying to find a holiday job," she informed him. "Ickfield and Wendover were hopeless and I'm not doing very well here, either. I've left my name at several places, but they didn't sound too hopeful."

He forced himself to respond. "What do you want a job for? Don't you get enough work at school?"

"I don't get paid for that! And until I make some friends here there's not all that much to do."

"Are you pleased to be back down here?" To his own ears he sounded unbelievably stilted but Vanessa didn't seem to notice. She shrugged.

"I don't mind really. I didn't want to come, because it meant leaving all my friends in Newcastle, but I like the house and village very much."

The pot of tea and the sundae arrived and he allowed himself to relax a little. Incredibly enough, he seemed to be coping all right.

"Mummy's gone to see Auntie Marion this afternoon," she remarked over the top of her ice-cream. "It was a pity you couldn't come on Sunday."

At the back of his mind an alarm bell rang. Julia would be sure to mention the invitation; he must have an excuse ready when Marion tackled him about it. His mind seemed to be split down the middle as neatly as Vanessa's banana, each half functioning entirely separately. How she was enjoying that revolting-looking ice! thought one, with avuncular affection. And: had that wide, soft mouth really been pressed so passionately against his? wondered the other.

His hand shook suddenly and he put his cup down. He mustn't allow himself to relax too much; his control was obviously very precarious. She had looked up as the cup rattled on the saucer and to distract her he spoke quickly, with no prior thought.

"Have you been up to that incredible Stone lately?"

Her eyes widened and for the space of a heartbeat he saw in their depths a hint of the mysterious *alter ego* that had so bewitched him. So there was some connection with the Stone! He remembered now it had been up there that her voice had first taken on that sultry, caressing note she had used in his room.

"Yes. I go most days."

"Don't you get tired of it?"

She said evasively, "There's quite a lot going on, sometimes. People go up there to watch the gliders. The take-off field reaches almost up to the Stone and when the wind's in the right direction I can sit and watch the man in the winch towing them along towards me. Nick wants to join the club. He went up in a glider the other day and can't talk of anything else!"

Brian was not interested in gliders. It was her reaction to his mention of the Stone which excited him. Momentary though it had been, that brief glimpse of knowledge in her eyes had convinced him that whatever explanation there might be for what had happened between them the other night, at least it really had taken place and was not some sick fancy of a diseased mind.

"Are you going straight home now?"

"Sorry?" He jolted his attention back to her.

"You don't have to go back to the office or anything?"

"No, why?"

"Would you be an absolute angel and give me a lift home? The queue for the bus will be enormous at this time of day. It's not very much out of your way, is it?"

"No. No, of course not." So his ordeal was to be prolonged still further.

The air outside was sultry and thunderous. He felt the prick of sweat on his skin and the glare from the pavements dazzled his tired eyes. Even Vanessa at his side drooped slightly in the excessive heat. The car when they reached it was standing in full sunshine and a blast of hot air greeted them when he opened the door.

As they inched their way up the narrow streets and into the one-way system of Market Square, Vanessa said idly, "Hilary starts work at the hospital next week. She's quite excited about it, but I'd hate it myself, poking about in people's insides!"

"I'm inclined to agree with you. What do you want to do when you leave school?"

"I don't know really. I'm not clever like Hilary and Nick, and I certainly don't want to go on taking exams all the time. Hilary never stops working, and once she starts at Rokeby she'll be on a twelve-hour day with only alternate weekends off."

"Just as well her fiancé's in Africa, then!" He glanced at

her but her head was turned away as she stared out of the window at the home-going crowds. "Do you like him?"

"Chris? Yes, he's all right. A bit studious and dedicated for me, though!"

"Are they planning to get married as soon as he comes home?"

"I don't know. I asked her the other day, but she was rather snappy about it. Actually –"

"Yes?"

"Nothing. It's just an idea I have, that's all."

She didn't volunteer anything further and he didn't press her, concentrating on seizing his chance to get on to the roundabout and out on the Stoke Mandeville road. This first encounter, which he'd been dreading since Friday, had after all passed off better than he could have hoped. Despite the agony he had endured over the last few days, nothing appeared to have changed outwardly between them. Vanessa was entirely at her ease, clearly regarding him in the same light as she had always done. It was abundantly obvious that she remembered nothing whatsoever about the incident. The appalling thing was that he himself could not forget it.

Adam closed the yellowing newspaper and leaned back in his chair, frowning thoughtfully. It was rather a disturbing story he'd unearthed on Vanessa's behalf and he was not at all sure how much of it he should pass on to an impressionable fifteen-year-old, especially since she had refused to hand over the enigmatic spell-stones which had figured so largely in the earlier tragedy. Certainly his own curiosity had been considerably aroused by several references made during the trial and he knew that for his own satisfaction he would have to follow them through. The problem was where to start. The newspaper archives which had produced so dramatic and unexpected a revelation about Clarissa Henry dealt solely in fact. What he needed now was a book on local folklore and superstitions, or perhaps – Louise! He suddenly remembered her mentioning that the magazine had once run a series on Chiltern villages including their local customs and legends. Her office was only a few doors down the street from where he was now.

He stood up resolutely, stacked all the papers he had been studying into one pile and went out into the main office of the newspaper.

"Thanks, Alan, that was invaluable! I'll do the same for you sometime!"

Alan Barnaby looked up briefly from his desk. raised a hand in acknowledgement, and turned to answer his ringing phone. Adam went quickly along the road and up the narrow twisting stairs into the warren of offices where Louise month by month produced her glossy magazine.

"Adam – hello! This is a pleasure! Sit down."

He seated himself across the desk from her. "I've come to ask for assistance, actually. You remember telling me about that series you were running on Chiltern villages?"

"Yes?"

"Was there by any chance an article on Ickfield?"

"I should think so. Yes, I'm sure there was."

"Would it be possible to have a look at it?"

"Of course, if we can find it. I'm not sure exactly when we did it."

"Perhaps I could search through some back copies? I've just spent a couple of hours down the road going over old newspaper records."

"Why the sudden interest in local history?"

"You remember on Thursday Vanessa Prior came to the shop just as we were leaving and said she had something to show me?"

Louise's eyes narrowed. "I remember."

"She'd found an old diary hidden in the summer-house. It was written in eighteen-eighty by Clarissa Henry."

"Clarissa –"

"Who, after a sensational murder trial at the Old Bailey,

was pronounced guilty but insane."

"Wow!" Louise gazed at him wide-eyed. "Of course, I remember now. I thought the name sounded familiar. And Vanessa found her diary! What a scoop! Is there a story in it for us?"

"There might be, later. During the trial Clarissa kept making the most intriguing references to the Druid Stone. Obviously her mind was unhinged by all the stories and superstitions she'd read about it. I know one or two of them myself but judging from her remarks there must be others. That's why I want to see the article, in case your reporter dug up a few more during her researches."

"Yes, it's beginning to come back to me. They were rather blood-curdling, some of them. I'm trying to think when it was we ran the series. Just a moment." She pulled the telephone towards her and spoke briefly to someone in the outer office, then looked across at Adam.

"It ran for eight months during '77. Shouldn't be too arduous to locate. Melanie's sent one of the juniors to look for it."

"Thanks very much."

Louise glanced across at him and then out of the window. "Does her sister know all about this?"

"Hilary? I've no idea. I suppose Vanessa might have told her, though she struck me as being a bit secretive about it."

"But you haven't mentioned it yourself?"

"I haven't seen her, except briefly when she opened the door on Saturday. But now that you mention it, I think perhaps I'd better have a word with her before I see Vanessa again."

"Why?"

"Well, you become quite involved with someone, you know, when you read her diary. I should think this is even more likely when it's someone roughly your own age, who actually used to live in your house. It's quite possible that Vanessa identified with her to some extent. To learn suddenly that she committed a particularly brutal murder and was proved insane could be quite traumatic."

"Yes, I see your point." She looked across at him reflectively and felt regret moving inside her. She knew he was glad of an excuse to see Hilary Prior again, and she also knew intuitively that each time he saw her, her own claim on him would lessen. Not that 'claim' was the right word. No strings, they had said bravely. The fact that Hilary was engaged did not weigh very heavily with Louise. She had seen the effect Adam had on girls in whom he had had no interest. Hilary Prior obviously did interest him, and Louise felt a stab of premature sympathy for her unknown fiancé.

A tap on the door brought the junior carrying the relevant copy of the magazine. It was dated April 1977. Eagerly Adam opened it and Louise came round to stand behind him, her hand on his shoulder.

"'Originally an Iron Age Settlement... arrow heads... flint –'" Adam flicked the pages impatiently. "'At the south-east end of the village, built on the lower slopes of the encircling Chilterns, stands Conningley, the attractive Georgian house which was once the home of the notorious murderess Clarissa Henry –'"

"I'll read this later," he said. "At the moment it's references to the Stone I'm looking for."

The telephone on the desk shrilled and Louise lifted it.

"Mr Harbourne to see you, Miss Dunne."

"Thank you. I'll be out in a minute." She replaced the receiver. "Damn, I'd forgotton I had this appointment."

Adam stood up. "I won't hold you up. Thanks a lot, Louise. This should be a great help."

She put her hand suddenly on his arm. "Adam – have dinner with me. Please. At the flat. It might be for the last time."

He looked at her with an amused smile. "You're not going psychic on me, are you?"

"I don't have to."

"An enigmatic remark! What does it mean?"

"Never mind. I'd very much like your company tonight, that's all."

"It'll be a pleasure." He bent forward and kissed her cheek. "Shall I call back here to collect you?"

"No, I have the car. I'll see you at the flat – six-thirty?"

"Fine. I'll look forward to it."

As Louise greeted the editor who had come to see her, her eyes went briefly past him to watch Adam leave the office. She knew that by the time he had reached the street he would have put her entirely from his mind – and she was right. He went straight across the road to a public call box. The Priors weren't in the directory and he had to dial Enquiries. It was hot in the small kiosk and the midday sun scorched the back of his neck through the glass. The ringing tone stopped and a voice said, "Hello?"

"Hilary?"

"Yes?"

"This is Adam Sandys. Good morning."

There was the briefest of pauses, and then she said, "I'm afraid Vanessa isn't in at the moment."

"It's you I was wanting to speak to. Did she happen to mention the diary she found?"

"Only in passing."

"She asked me to go through it for her, and quite honestly it's a bit of a shaker."

"In what way?"

"Certain things have come to light about the girl who wrote it, and I'm not sure how much it would be wise to tell Vanessa. I wondered if you could advise me?"

"I'll try. What did you find out?"

"It's rather a long story; too long for a phone call. Perhaps we could have a drink together and discuss it?"

"This evening?" She sounded a little doubtful.

Louise: damn! "I'm afraid I can't manage this evening. How about tomorrow?"

"I think that would be all right."

"May I call for you about eight?"

"Fine. What shall I tell Vanessa?"

"Just say I want your medical advice about something! In a way it's quite true."

She said slowly, "That sounds most intriguing. Very well, Adam. Eight o'clock tomorrow."

He pushed open the door of the kiosk, gave a broad smile to the girl who was waiting outside and, leaving her staring wistfully after him, strode down the road in search of lunch and the opportunity to read through the magazine.

Nine

There was a severe electrical storm that night. It started in the late evening and Brian stood for an hour or more at his bedroom window watching sheet lightning play across the hills while the thunder rolled echoingly around, tossing the sound from one ridge to another. He thought of the Stone on the hill above Conningley, imagined it recharging itself, storing up further supplies of current. It would be an awesome sight on this storm-ridden night, with its impassive face turned to the glancing rain and the lightning spotlighting it from time to time in an unearthly glow. A wild sense of excitement began to build inside him, irrational, primitive, conjured up by the timeless majesty of the storm, and eventually he could bear the confines of the house no longer.

Silently he opened his bedroom door and paused for a moment on the landing. From behind Miss Fergusson's door came a gentle, rhythmic snoring, from behind Marion's, silence. Was she too awake, listening to the storm? He did not take the trouble to find out but made his way barefoot down the stairs, through the sleeping hall and into the kitchen. The black cat asleep on top of the boiler opened an amber eye which glowed at him across the dark room like a cyclops. He unbolted the back door and stepped outside.

Instantly he was drenched by the breath-stopping coldness of the rain and a savage exhilaration seized hold of him. Leaving the door open behind him he set off down the path, the rain streaming from his beard and every nerve quivering to the stimuli which bombarded him on all sides. The silk of his pyjamas was plastered against his body like a second skin and this near-nakedness intensified his affinity with the primeval nature of the night. How many years was it, he wondered bemusedly, since he had walked barefoot over wet grass, feeling the warmth of the earth beneath the surface cold? He stood in the middle of the lawn, head flung back, eyes closed against the silver arrows of rain which stung his skin and soaked the thick mat of his hair. And suddenly, between one second and the next, the euphoric exultation drained away.

Dazedly he opened his eyes and stared about him, at the silvered lawn pock-marked with his footprints, at the writhing trees and humped black shape of the house, and a fit of uncontrollable shivering took hold of him, rattling his teeth with merciless ferocity. What in the name of heaven was he doing, out in a thunderstorm in his pyjamas?

He turned and stumbled back to the house, head bent. The open door was banging backwards and forwards and the floor inside was soaked with rain. He pushed the door shut, his cold wet fingers fumbling awkwardly with the bolt, which tore a wedge of skin from his finger. Leaving a trail of wet footprints, he went back upstairs and into the bathroom, where he stripped off the cold clinging pyjamas and rubbed his body down briskly to restore the circulation, towelling hair and beard in an almost phrenetic desire to be rid of the memory of that temporary madness. The depths of the airing cupboard revealed a clean pair of pyjamas and these he thankfully put on, leaving the soaked pair in a heap on the floor. The thunder was dying away now and only an occasional flare lit the dark window-pane. Miss Fergusson's gentle snores reached him again as he opened the door of his room, and with an odd sense of narrowly averted disaster, he went shakily inside.

Adam, too, had been listening to the storm, his arm encircling Louise as she slept. The evening had not really been a success. His mind had been fixed on the research he'd been engaged in all day, and though at first Louise seemed interested, he realized that she'd begun to resent his preoccupation, not least, he suspected, because it was tenuously connected with the Priors. Or perhaps, if he was honest, not so tenuously. Making love to Louise he had been treacherously aware of his thoughts turning repeatedly to Hilary and their proposed evening together, and he had striven to overcome the guilt of this awareness with extra tenderness. At the end, he knew, she had been crying, though neither of them referred to it. 'It might be for the last time', she had said when she invited him, and with a sense of gentle regret he realized now that it was. He and Louise had been right for each other over the last two years. He'd been able to help her over her infatuation with Jeremy Nailham, she had provided him with an alibi whenever the occasional girl – usually, he thought with a wry smile, introduced to him by his mother – had sought to involve him. He had not wanted to be involved, and that had been the reason for the success of the relationship. No strings of any kind; a deep affection for each other, without any of the responsibilities or jealousies a closer commitment would have entailed. The affection was still there, but its nature had subtly altered. He hoped very much that their friendship would prove strong enough to survive the partial severing.

She stirred beside him, turned her head and kissed his shoulder.

"I must be going," he said softly.

"No, not yet. You can't go home through the storm."

"It's easing off now." He moved his lips over her face and

she drew his mouth to hers. It was a long, long kiss and they both knew it was good-bye. When it was finished she said unsteadily,

"I was right, wasn't I? It's over."

"Only part of it," he said gently.

She gave a choked little laugh. "I can be a sister to you?"

"I promise never to think of you in that light! Darling Louise, it's been a wonderful two years."

"Yes." Her fingers moved lingeringly over his chest and arm. "We're lucky it lasted so long."

"You'll still have dinner with me from time to time?"

"Not here. There'd be too many memories."

"Not here, then. We've no regrets, have we?"

Only that it didn't last longer, she thought privately. Aloud, she said bravely, "No regrets." She wanted to ask him about Hilary, to probe this wound which had no right to be a wound at all, but she knew it would be to no avail. There was nothing he could tell her, for nothing had happened. He had been completely honest with her. She knew he was meeting Hilary tomorrow – this evening, now – to discuss the diary. And because of that meeting, even though nothing might come of it, their own association must end.

Gently he disengaged his arm and started to dress. She watched him with pain-dulled eyes. The rain still drummed on the window, and she realized desolately that even when he had gone she could not allow herself the luxury of tears. Swollen eyes would cause lifted eyebrows at the office in the morning, and a dedicated career girl had no right to shed them anyway.

"May I take the magazine with me? I'll let you have it back as soon as possible."

The beastly magazine, which had been instrumental in taking him away from her. "Yes, of course."

He stood looking down at her. "You'll be all right, won't you?"

"Of course," she said again.

"If ever I can be of help, you only have –"

"Please, Adam! If you're going, go quickly!"

"Yes – I'm sorry." He bent and brushed his lips against hers. "Good-bye, Louise. Take care."

"Good-bye." The word stuck in her throat, was only whispered to the empty room as the door closed behind him.

"Did you hear someone was struck by lightning up on the hill last night?" Nick demanded excitedly as he came in to lunch. "They were talking about it at the club."

"I'm surprised anyone was up there in that storm," Julia commented, handing him his plate.

"It was a courting couple – they're out in all weathers! But it was before the rain started anyway, about eleven o'clock, apparently. Don't they say lightning's more dangerous, without rain?"

"Were they seriously hurt?"

"Not really. They were up by the Stone, and the boy swears there wasn't any lightning at that particular moment, but of course there must have been. Perhaps they were too busy to notice it! He says the girl just put out her hand to touch the Stone and immediately fell to the ground."

"Is she in hospital?" Hilary asked with professional interest.

"Yes, with shock and minor burns. I bet they won't go up there again in a hurry!"

Vanessa smiled secretly to herself. Though no-one would believe him, she knew the boy had been speaking the truth. The Stone would not need the assistance of lightning to strike down any intruder who came too close. She excused herself as soon as she'd finished her meal and, going up to her room, retrieved the spell-stones from their hiding-place and turned them over in her hands. She had taken them up to the Stone that morning and laid them for several minutes in the shallow hollow where they belonged. Now they too

were recharged with the earth-force which flowed so
strongly through the Stone. She stared down at the
tolmaen, wondering whether to slip it round her neck, but
she refrained. It was not to be put on lightly, like an
unimportant trinket. She must wait until she received
specific instructions, as she had last night. Last night it had
been necessary to reach out, to transmit the will of the
Stone across the storm-torn hills to the valley below as a
demonstration of total mental control. It was necessary for
him to be made aware of it, as he had previously been
forced to accept his physical subjugation. Make ready,
Bran the Blessed, your time approaches.

Vanessa lifted her head, frowning slightly. What had she
been thinking? The remembered confusion clouded her
mind. Seconds before, she had known exactly what it was
all about; now, the thread was lost again. The prickling in
her hands grew stronger and she tipped the stones back into
their bag. Briefly she thought of Adam Sandys and hoped
he would stand by his promise not to mention them. No-
one else must handle them now. Each handling would
necessarily dilute the current and that must remain at full
strength until she needed it.

Adam said, "I suggest we go to the Green Man. Do you
know it? It's only a mile away across the fields and makes a
very pleasant walk, though the grass may still be wet after
last night's rain."

"That doesn't matter. I've been indoors all day reading
through my notes. I'd love a walk." She glanced down at
the document case he was carrying. "That looks very
official, for an evening in a country pub!"

"It was mainly to conceal the diary in case I happened to
see Vanessa, but there are a few other things I want to show
you as well."

"What is all this about the diary? I don't quite see how it
can affect Van."

"Did she tell you anything at all about it?"

"Only that she found it in the summer-house and it had been written about a hundred years ago by someone who lived at Conningley."

"There's a lot more to it than that. She asked me to find out about the family for her, and as it's turned out I'm thankful she didn't try to do so herself."

"Why?"

Adam unlatched the five-barred gate leading to the field and stood aside for her to pass through.

"Because," he answered deliberately, "the girl who wrote the diary was afterwards convicted of murder."

Hilary stopped and stared at him. "*Murder*?"

"Yes. Apparently she chopped someone's head off, up there on the hill. And that, oddly enough, ties in with a whole host of legends about that Stone of yours. I've been reading an article on the village which was published a few years ago. It was pretty thoroughly researched and various sources were quoted for further reference if the reader was interested. I was, and spent the afternoon at the County Library tracking them down. It seems that for some reason people over the years have reacted very strongly towards the Stone. They either become obsessed by it, or it terrifies them to the point of madness."

He paused, choosing his words with care so as not to alarm her. "It's possible that a young girl like your sister could become susceptible to it if she hears too much about it. She doesn't go up there often, does she?"

"Not as far as I know. She did take Brian one Sunday –"

"The man she calls Uncle Bran?"

"That's right."

"You know, even that's odd, in the circumstances. There was a Celtic god called Bran."

"So I believe. Van regaled me with some horrible story about his head living on after he was dead."

"Exactly. The severed head. We keep coming back to it all the time: Bran, the skull in the well, Clarissa Henry – and the Stone."

"What has the Stone to do with it?"

"One of the less savoury legends is that periodically, roughly every hundred years or so, it demands the offering of a human head."

"Oh, now look! You're not seriously –"

"It's serious enough, Hilary, if only because Clarissa Henry believed it. She mentioned it in the diary and again at the trial. That was why she inveigled her doctor to the Stone and chopped his head off. Legend can be self-perpetuating, you know."

She stared at him wide-eyed. "Oh God!" she said softly.

"The Stone seems to be literally blood-thirsty. There are dozens of records of it being regularly anointed with blood until fairly recently, despite all the church's attempts to stamp out the custom."

The wet grass brushed against her legs and she shivered instinctively. They walked for a few minutes in silence until they came to the crest of the field and could look away to their right at the huddled roofs and farms of Ickfield. To the left a small wood clothed the gentle slopes of the hill, while directly ahead a panorama lay spread before them of patchwork fields, scattered cottages and in the distance the white thread of a road.

"This is part of the Icknield Way," Adam said. "It always gives me an odd feeling to know men have been walking along it for over five thousand years. I read somewhere it was already old when Stonehenge was built."

"And the Druid Stone was standing then, too. You know, I haven't even seen it yet. After all this I must certainly go and have a look." She glanced across at him. "If the sacrifice is demanded every hundred years and the diary is a hundred years old, does that mean we're just about due for another one?"

"Presumably. According to the records the pattern always seems to follow the same lines. Towards the end of the 'dormant' period the Stone begins to get restless and for a year or two there are an increasing number of unexplained reports about it – odd happenings in the vicinity – that kind of thing. All this builds up to the climax, after which, 'glutted with the sacrifice' as the book charmingly puts it, the Stone becomes quiescent for another century."

"You sound as though you almost believe it yourself!" Hilary said with a little laugh. "So does that mean Clarissa Henry was simply the last in a long line of – perpetrators?"

"Exactly."

"What other form have these 'climaxes' taken in the past?"

"Incredibly enough, they have all been decapitations, which is a sufficiently unusual means of death to give added point to the legend, wouldn't you say?"

They had reached the bottom of the field. Adam opened another gate and they came out on to the country lane that they had seen from the hill. A hundred yards along it stood a picturesque little pub with a garden alongside in which tables and chairs were laid out.

"There's quite a pleasant bar parlour, if you'd rather go inside."

"No, let's stay in the garden, provided it doesn't get too cool."

He steered her over to a table by the hedge which would catch the last of the evening sunshine and she settled herself in a chair while he went to collect their drinks. When he returned, she said thoughtfully, "A girl received a shock up near the Stone during the storm last night."

"You mean she was struck by lightning?"

"The boy who was with her says not, that she just put out her hand to touch it and fell to the ground with burns and shock."

"That does happen sometimes near these ancient stones. Apparently it can actually be dangerous to go too close to certain of them at certain times, possibly because the brain could become overcharged. They say you either go mad or become a poet – as though one alternative was as bad as the other!"

"But what kind of current could that be?"

"I've no idea. Some cosmic energy, perhaps. You're more of a scientist than I am."

"Then you wouldn't regard the incident last night as being one of the expected unusual happenings up there?"

"It could be, I suppose, though it wouldn't be unique and the fact that there was lightning about rather detracts from the theory. Of course, there was also that story your brother told of the little boy who said the Stone had hit him. Again, it was completely uncorroborated, but these things always are."

He unzipped the document case he had brought with him. "If you can suspend your disbelief a little longer I think these'll interest you. Firstly, here's the diary, with the transcribed version pinned to it. I worked on it all day Sunday and persuaded one of the girls at the shop to type it out for me. Incidentally, I came across something else rather strange. Isn't that woman who works for you a Mrs Hare?"

"Yes?"

"Well, there's one in the diary too. It was she who kept plying Clarissa with details of the legend, and who later gave her the spell-stones."

"The what?"

Adam hesitated, mindful of, though regretting, his promise to Vanessa. " A collection of small stones which was normally kept in the hollow of the Druid Stone. They were used as extensions of it – portable stones for healing, warding off evil, even, in some cases, for hypnotism."

"Good heavens! And this Mrs Hare had them? That's quite a coincidence, isn't it?"

"I'd have thought it was worth mentioning, certainly, but curiously enough Vanessa didn't. She must have noticed it – after all, she'd read the relevant part of the diary. But she just referred to her as 'a woman in the village'. I wonder why."

"Van has some kind of hang-up about Mrs Hare. I've noticed it myself. She never speaks either to or about her if she can avoid it. I wondered if she half-believed Nick's wild theories about her being a witch! It's strange, though, that the name should crop up twice like that. It's not all that common, surely."

"That's what I thought so I looked it up in the phone book. There were about thirty of them listed so it's not as rare as all that. I don't mind telling you I was quite relieved! Even so, there are still one or two puzzling connections with the name. For a start, there was a hare engraved on one of the spell-stones, which we know were at one time in the first Mrs Hare's possession. It seems that hares are becoming as numerous as severed heads!"

"And that little boy saw one – a 'big bunny', remember? It was to stop him chasing it that he said the Stone hit him!" She gave a rather embarrassed little laugh. "It's easy to see how these superstitions build up, isn't it? Just one chance happening on top of another, and before you know it you're in danger of believing it yourself!"

Adam looked at her thoughtfully but did not reply and after a moment she picked up the diary. "Won't this be quite valuable?"

"I should say it must be unique. Not many murderesses write a full account of their crime."

"She actually wrote about that?"

"Indeed she did, and in a particularly unpleasant way. It's rather chilling to see how her character changes as you read through the book and her fantasies begin to take over. She becomes obsessed with people's heads – trying to decide on a suitable one, perhaps! – and goes into long descriptions about the shape of ears and the width of foreheads. Knowing what was coming, it made decidedly uncomfortable reading, I can tell you. Poor Clarissa: it was as well for her that the plea of insanity had been recognized by then."

"I'm not so sure. From what I've heard of Victorian

asylums I should think hanging was preferable."

"Perhaps. Just listen to this." He picked up the typescript.

"'November 1st. All Saints' Day, yet it was surely a demon that manifested itself to me. I was paying my daily visit to the Stone and did not at once perceive the still shape crouched in the shadow of it, seeming like a rock itself save for the pale, flat eyes regarding me so fixedly. I believed I should fall insensible to the ground, but as I leaned half-fainting against the Stone its pulsing life force flowed into my body and restored me. I collected myself and looked again but the creature was gone, leaving behind in the muddy grass a set of foot-prints resembling those of a beast, with pad marks clearly discernible.'"

Hilary drew a deep breath. "I don't think I'll be reading that in bed tonight."

"No, I shouldn't. You see why I hesitated about handing it back to Vanessa? Incidentally, Clarissa made use of this 'elemental' as she called it to get the doctor up to the Stone. She insisted it was hiding behind the altar slab and when, humouring her, he bent forward to look – zap! as the comics used to say. She must have had the axe hidden up there ready. Shades of Lizzie Borden! Believe me, it reads like a gothic novel!" He looked at her with a smile. "But I'm forgetting my duties! Would you like another drink?"

"I feel I need one, after all this!"

"Same again?"

She nodded and as he went back inside the bar she picked up the other book he had left on the table: *Folklore and Legend in South Bucks.* He'd marked a place in it with a piece of paper and she opened it at the indicated page.

'Through the ages' she read, 'there have always been the same two parts to be played in the drama of the Druid Stone, that of the Priest or Priestess – usually the latter – and that of the Victim. Who knows how these roles come to be cast? Are they, one wonders, predestined to seek each other out for that end? Is their fate decreed from birth, and if so, which birth? For one of the more fanciful suggestions put forward is that this long list of Priests and Victims – Katherine and Richard, Georgina and Peregrine, Clarissa and Dr Harvey – is in fact an endless reincarnation of the same two souls, compelled because of some past wickedness to re-enact their macabre drama throughout eternity.'

Adam's shadow came between her and the setting sun and she jumped.

"The style's pretty flowery," he commented, setting down the glasses, "but it makes fascinating reading, doesn't it? Lindsay Pendle, who wrote the magazine article, was considerably more guarded. You can take them both back with you if you like and compare them, but I'd be grateful if I could keep the diary for a little longer. Incidentally, if you decide to sell it later it would probably be of considerable interest to psychologists and criminologists, not to mention collectors in general."

"What will you tell Vanessa when she asks about it?"

"I'll stall as long as I can, but of course if she insists I'll have to give it to her. She might well be tougher than we think."

"All the same, thank you for not handing it back to her regardless. I can't help feeling it would upset her."

"But it doesn't upset you? Not even the slightest hint of uneasiness?"

"Well, Clarissa's story is horrifying, but as you say, she was mentally ill." She looked across at him. "You don't really expect me to believe it all, do you? Blood-thirsty stones and earth currents and transmogrification into hares?"

"Not exactly, no, though a lot of the stories have been historically verified." He smiled slightly. "You must make allowances for me, Hilary. I was brought up on these stories and I'm quite defensive about them."

"Folklore fascinates me, too. After all, it gives a unique insight into the growth of a nation's character."

"Quite so," he said dryly. "Thank God for the cold, clear

light of science! I'd become so steeped in all this over the last few days that I was beginning to lose my sense of proportion. Thank you for hearing me out so patiently."

Her eyes fell to the book in her hand. She knew her reaction had disappointed him and she was sorry, but how could she, a doctor in the late twentieth century, admit to a crawling sensation of fear when she read of vengeful stones and elementals crouching in their shadows?'

She reached for her glass and the last rays of the sun struck blue fire from the sapphire on her finger. Adam's own fingers tightened on his glass and he drained it quickly. The sky was rose-washed now, pricked with the first stars, and over the hill hung the golden sickle of a new moon. There was an ache in her throat but she didn't care to analyse it.

"Perhaps we'd better start walking back," she said quietly, and followed Adam across the grass as he handed in their empty glasses. Above her the inn sign swung creakingly in a sudden stir of breeze and she looked up to see the gargoyle-like head of the legendary Green Man with a vine growing out of his mouth. This time she couldn't quite suppress a little shudder of recoil.

"Another pointer to the nation's character!" Adam said lightly, noticing the direction of her gaze. "He even appears on the ends of the pews in Ickfield Church. Did they really believe they'd stamped out the Old Religion, do you suppose?"

She didn't reply, merely pulled her woollen jacket more closely about her, and he regretted the remark. Perhaps she felt he was mocking her, whereas really it was himself he mocked. He took her elbow to guide her across the road and since, just inside the field, she almost tripped on the uneven ground, he retained hold of her arm. Strung in the distance the isolated lights of the farmhouses lay scattered like fallen stars and somewhere in the woods to their right an owl hooted suddenly.

To break the lengthening silence between them, she said

awkwardly, "I feel I should thank you on Vanessa's behalf for all the trouble you've taken. You must have given up a lot of time to check all those references."

"I enjoyed it. Incidentally, I'd be glad to have the books back when you've read them."

"Of course."

The walk home seemed farther than on the outward journey and they no longer knew what to say to each other. Adam was conscious of a feeling of anticlimax. Without being sure what he'd expected of the evening, it had not gone quite as he'd hoped and he was uncomfortably aware that the initial attraction he'd felt for Hilary had deepened considerably. It had been a mistake to contact her. He should have stuck to his original intention of trying to put her out of his mind.

They reached the main road at last and ahead of them, beyond the dark circle of the green, glowed the lights of Conningley. At the gate they stopped and his hand fell from her arm.

"Thank you for agreeing to come this evening," he said formally.

"Thanks for asking me."

"I'll – no doubt see you around."

She smiled a little. "You might not. From Monday I'll be working flat out at the hospital."

"You have days off, surely?"

"Alternate weekends, I hope. That's all."

"Then I'm even more grateful that you spared me this evening."

She couldn't see his face in the half-light but his voice had a rather clipped quality. She said quietly, "Good-night, Adam" and walked away from him up the drive. She didn't turn round, but she was almost sure he stood looking after her until the front door closed behind her.

The sound of the television was coming from the sitting-room, but she couldn't face her family just then. She called brightly, "I'm in! Good-night!", waited for their answering call, and went straight up the stairs. And as she closed her bedroom door behind her, to her utter consternation she burst into tears.

Ten

"Like to make up a foursome for the flicks tonight?" David Sandys asked his brother at breakfast the next day.

"I don't think so, thanks."

"But Robert Redford's one of Louise's favourites!"

"Then I'm afraid she'll have to make her own arrangements to see him."

"Oh? You two had a row?"

"No," Adam answered deliberately, folding his napkin. "We have not had a row, but since you're so curious, we've decided not to see quite as much of each other in future."

"I'm very glad to hear it," his mother said decidedly. "You've wasted enough time on that girl and I never cared for her. Much too hard-headed and businesslike, in my opinion."

"She isn't hard at all, dear Mother, and I'm still very fond of her, but we felt the time had come to make a break."

"You mean you did," David said shrewdly.

"She agreed with me. It was all very amicable."

"Anyone else in mind?"

"No," said Adam shortly. "May we please change the subject?"

"I don't know what's the matter with you two," Mrs Sandys remarked with a sigh. "I'm beginning to wonder if I shall ever get you off my hands!"

Over the Conningley breakfast table, Julia was asking her children whether they would be accompanying her and

Gavin to the party the following evening.

"I suppose so," Vanessa said without enthusiasm.

"I'm glad, darling. Hilary? One last mad fling before you disappear into those sterilized corridors?"

"How could I resist it? Actually, it'll probably be pretty hard going. We're bound to have grown away from them all."

"You'll find plenty to talk about, I'm sure."

"I think I'll give Steve a ring," Nick said hopefully. "There's quite a good film on in Aylesbury."

"No," Julia said firmly. "If you'd had something definite arranged it would be different, but as it is you can come with us. Anyway, it's as a family that they want to see us after all this time. The Laidlaw boys are sure to be there; you used to be very friendly with them."

Hilary pushed in her chair and left them to their dicussion. She didn't particularly want to go to the party, but at least it would pass the evening. The post dropped through the letter-box as she reached the hall. Still nothing from Chris, but a letter from Sally, who had been with her in Italy. She took it up to her room and stood aimlessly looking about her. The sooner Monday came and she could throw herself into some strenuous work, the better. She was not very happy with her own thoughts at the moment.

With a sigh she opened a drawer and took out the book, the magazine and the typescript of the diary which Adam had given her, and, pulling a chair over to the window, she began to read them.

When, two hours later, she had finished, the balance of her outlook had shifted considerably. 'Not the slightest hint of uneasiness?' Adam had asked her, and she knew now what he had meant. There was a nagging foreboding at the back of her mind and no amount of logical, twentieth-century common sense would remove it. Her imagination swung with sick fascination between the age-old mysteries of blood sacrifices and the distorted ravings of poor, mad Clarissa who, a hundred years ago, had played her part in fulfilling them.

As Adam had warned her, the deterioration in the mind of the diarist had been peculiarly horrifying as she changed almost imperceptibly from the gently reared girl who laughed with her friend about 'Mistress Hare's' rantings, to the cold-blooded murderess unequivocally convinced of the role she had to play.

'He has a strong neck,' she wrote of Dr Augustus Harvey. 'Would that I could be sure of severing it at one stroke! I dream repeatedly of mismanaging the task, and of the doctor chasing after me with his head fixed only by a thread. Yet despite these moments of doubt, I know in my heart that all will be well. The Stone will be at my side and will endow me with all the strength that I require.'

Hilary dropped the typescript to the floor and turned instead to the magazine, flicking through the pages and passing unseeingly over Lady So-and-so in her rose garden and Miss Somebody Else whose engagement had just been announced. And so she came again to the article. *Ickfield and its Druid Stone*. 'For some reason,' Adam had said, 'people over the years have reacted very strongly to the Stone.' And she herself had not even taken the trouble to walk up the hill to look at it.

She stood up suddenly, pushed the books and papers back out of sight and set off to rectify the omission. It was a dull day, cool and overcast, and as she came out on to the hill above the garden she wished she'd brought a jacket with her. There was quite a well-worn track, she noticed, leading up from the garden gate. Who, or what, had flattened the grasses by its frequent passing? Or had they simply been crushed by the weight of the Stone itself when it came to drink from the well on Midsummer Day?

Despite herself, she glanced back over her shoulder. The path fell away behind her, unrevealing and deserted, and with an exclamation of impatience at her own timidity she hurried on. When finally she reached the top of the hill she was aware of a sense of anticlimax. The Stone loomed in front of her, majestic certainly and unbelievably old, but so exactly like the pictures in both the book and the magazine that she felt no impact at all. Further along the ridge of the hill she could see the cluster of buildings which formed Nick's beloved gliding club, with some of the machines lying in the grass like grounded albatrosses. But, she reminded herself, it was the Stone she had come to see.

Slowly and critically she walked round it, studying it carefully. It was perhaps fifteen feet at its highest point, and about eight across at its base. However the full height existed for only half the width, leaving a long, flattish surface about three feet from the ground. This, Hilary thought with a shudder of distaste, must be the so-called altar over which poor Dr Harvey had peered to see the mythical creature his patient insisted was there.

Reluctantly she went nearer, conscientiously searching for the features she had read about. At the back of the 'altar' where the Stone reared up to its full height was a shallow saucer-shaped depression. It was here presumably that the mysterious spell-stones had been kept and where also the libations of blood had been regularly poured.

With a conscious effort, Hilary forced herself to lean forward and feel round the inner surface of the hollow with her fingers. To her unspeakable horror she was instantly aware of an undeniable stickiness and snatched her hand away, staring at her fingers almost as though she expected them to be coated with blood. But nothing was visible on them and when she cautiously sniffed at the unseen substance, a faint unpleasant odour reached her nostrils reminiscent of sour milk.

Almost fearfully she put out her hand again, laying the flat of her palm against the uneven surface. No tingling current reached out to her, no violent shock sent her, like the girl in the thunderstorm, crashing to the ground. Certain people, Adam had said, at certain times of the year. Either she was not one of them or the time wasn't right. She surprised in herself a faint sense of disappointment. So this

was the notorious Druid Stone. Had she not heard and read
about it in advance, she would not have been unduly
interested in it. Still, this Stone, however innocent it might
be in itself – and how could an inanimate piece of rock be
otherwise? – had undoubtedly, by the stories woven about
it, caused the death of at least one man and, if the stories
stretching back across the centuries were to be believed,
quite possibly, a dozen or more beside.

She stood looking silently up at it. Well, I've seen you, she
thought, and you've seen me. I don't think we've anything
more to say to each other. She started back across the grass,
but just before the path dipped below the level of the hill
she turned like Lot's wife to look back, and like a
corresponding pillar of salt, implacable and immovable, the
Druid Stone seemed to stare back at her. She was conscious
of a ridiculous feeling of relief when, a moment later, the
path took her out of its sight.

Odd, how clearly defined this track was, she thought
again. It must be used quite regularly, possibly by animals.
Hares, for instance? She smiled wryly at the thought. It was
only as she reached the garden gate once more that she
saw the track did not after all finish there. It skirted round
the wall and continued down the hill, and after a second's
hesitation, Hilary followed it. There was a small copse
growing quite close against the walls but the track went on
confidently through the trees, last year's leaves trodden
firmly down where they had fallen across it. It had moved
away from the boundaries of Conningley now and was
descending at an angle which would presumably bring it
out on the main road beyond Green Crescent. Perhaps then
this was the path used by people going up the hill from the
village and was not as sinister as she'd begun to imagine.
But as she reached that point in her deductions she
emerged on the far side of the trees. The slope of the hill
continued for a further two hundred yards or so and ended
at the back garden walls of a row of small cottages facing on
to the main road. And in the garden of one of them,

hanging out some washing, was Mrs Hare. Hilary stood watching her for some minutes. Then, abandoning her intention of continuing to the end of the path and returning home along the road, she turned and made her way carefully back up the hill.

When the Priors set out for the party the following evening, Hilary had still not returned the books to Adam. She could of course have handed them in at the antique shop even if he was not there, but she felt she owed it to him to admit her own disquiet after reading them, and it would not be easy to do so in a shop full of customers. Taking them round to his home on Sunday might afford her a better chance, unless, of course, she reminded herself carefully, he was out somewhere with his girl friend.

Haddenham church with the duck-pond in front of it was just as they remembered and Julia felt a spurt of nostalgia as they passed the house where they'd once lived. Minutes later, Gavin had drawn up outside the Pembrooks' home and Mike was coming down the path to greet them.

"You're wearing very well, darling!" Linda commented, surveying Julia critically after the initial exclamations were over. "It's hard to believe these enormous offspring are yours! I hope you'll feel the same about me, when you see the twins! Come inside, everyone. Tracy's brought her sister along, since she's spending the weekend with them, but I think you know everybody else."

The room seemed full of people, but the first whom Julia recognized, to her considerable surprise, were Mr and Mrs Denton, from whom they had bought Conningley.

"You've met, of course." Linda took her arm and led her over to them. "Isn't it a coincidence? Tom works in Mike's office, and it was only by chance that we discovered they used to live in your house. We thought it might be pleasant for you all to meet again socially."

"Are you settling down all right?" Mary Denton enquired. "I suppose you feel quite at home by now."

Julia had only time to make a smiling assent before Tracy Turner came hurrying over to greet her. "Julia, you look wonderful! How marvellous to see you again! I've been meaning to get in touch ever since you moved in – is it really three weeks? – but you know how it is, and of course I knew I'd see you here. By the way, this is my younger sister, Louise. She's staying with us for a few days."

Across the room Vanessa touched Hilary's arm and murmured in a low voice: "See that girl talking to Mummy? She's the one who was with Adam when I called at the shop."

Hilary turned quickly at the same moment as Louise glanced in her direction and across the room their eyes met briefly before both of them looked away. Was Adam here too, then? Hilary wondered in confusion, and found herself hoping not. She had no wish to meet him in the company of the girl over there.

Louise too had been startled to realise who Hilary was. Tracy had told her the party was being held to welcome back some old friends but no names had been mentioned until her introduction to Julia. Immediately she scanned the room and caught sight of Vanessa, realizing with a sinking heart that the girl with her must surely be Hilary. No wonder Adam had been preoccupied since meeting her. She found herself wondering ruefully how their evening had progressed.

Nick meanwhile had also received a surprise, in the unbelievable transformation five years had wrought in the Pembrook twins. Amanda, pert and pretty, was thoroughly enjoying his discomfiture, her arm firmly linked through that of Bruce Laidlaw.

"Well, you've grown, Nick I'll say that for you. But have you grown any *nicer*, that's the point! You really were the most ghastly little boy! Claire and I couldn't abide you, and Mother always insisted on asking you to our parties!"

Nick, flushed, doggedly held his own. "You were pretty awful yourself! When you came to our house I had to let you play with my trains and you nearly always managed to break one." He glanced at Bruce, irritated by the smirk on his face. Had he any real claim to Amanda, or was her clinging to him just an act?

"There's dancing in the next room," she remarked, and her eyes went mischievously from Nick to Bruce, who obediently led her through. Claire, always the quieter twin, touched Nick's arm.

"Don't let her tease you," she advised. "She was quite excited at the thought of seeing you again."

Nick felt a warm rush of gratitude towards her and a sudden lift of heart. "Thanks for telling me. Shall we go and dance too?"

"Why not?"

As he steered her through he was planning the best way of prising Amanda away from Bruce.

Julia found Mrs Denton at her side again. "How are you finding the industrious Mrs Hare?" she enquired, her eyes curiously on Julia's face.

"A paragon, as you told me."

"I couldn't fault her work, certainly, but she's rather an odd woman, isn't she? To be honest I hadn't intended having a daily when we moved to Conningley, but she arrived on the doorstep out of the blue and almost begged me to engage her. In fact she was so anxious, and asked such a modest wage that I had the feeling if I'd still refused to take her on she'd have come for nothing! And it's a funny thing, but the dog never liked her. He's normally such a friendly little thing, but that woman seemed to terrify him. He cowered in a corner every time she came into a room, though I'm quite sure she never touched him."

"Perhaps she disliked him all the same. Animals can often tell, can't they?" Vanessa had come over to join them and Julia added, "Mrs Denton was asking how we're settling down."

The girl looked at her with sudden interest. "Have you any children, Mrs Denton?"

"No, no I'm afraid we haven't. The house was really too big for us."

"Why did you board up the well, then?"

If it hadn't been so ludicrous, Julia would have sworn that a look of fear crossed the woman's face. "It – it seemed rather unhygienic and – we were afraid of Toby falling in. He's our little poodle."

"He couldn't have climbed that high, surely, and Mrs Hare told me he never went in the garden anyway."

There was no mistaking the hunted look in Mrs Denton's eyes and Julia put in quickly, "Darling, there's really no call to grill poor Mrs Denton like that! If she wanted to board up the well there was no reason why she shouldn't do so. I can't imagine why you didn't leave it as it was."

Mary Denton's tongue flicked over her lips. "You – you didn't uncover it?"

"I'm afraid she did, the first chance she had."

"In – in time for Midsummer Day?"

A smile flooded over Vanessa's face. "Exactly! I thought you'd understand!"

Julia looked in bewilderment from the white face of the older woman to her daughter's triumphant one. "Midsummer? But why –?"

"For the Stone to come and drink, of course!" Vanessa said. And laughed. Mrs Denton stared at her for a long moment and then, with a muttered excuse, hurried from the room. Julia looked after her in amazement.

"What on earth was all that about? Did I miss something? She seems really upset."

"Never mind about her," Vanessa said without interest. "Auntie said supper's nearly ready. I came over to tell you."

In the dining-room Louise found herself standing next to Hilary and they exchanged rather cautious smiles. "Did you find the magazine interesting?" she enquired as they helped themselves to the buffet.

Hilary looked at her blankly. "I beg your pardon?"

"The magazine, with the article on your village. Didn't Adam show it to you?"

"Oh – I'm sorry! Yes, of course. I didn't realize – is it yours?"

"I'm the editor actually, but he borrowed it from our archives."

"I see. Yes, it was fascinating."

"And are you going to pass the information on to your sister?"

Hilary glanced at her in surprise. Adam had obviously discussed the whole matter with this girl, and for some reason she resented it. "I haven't decided yet. I'll probably try to tone it down a bit. Some of the details are pretty gruesome."

Rona Laidlaw came up behind them and started to fill her plate. "I hear your fiancé's abroad for a whole year, Hilary. That is bad luck!"

For me, too, thought Louise wryly. So that was why there had been no sign of him. Rona turned to her.

"And how's that dishy young man of yours? You should have brought him along this evening!"

She might have done, too, if it hadn't been for Wednesday night, and what would have happened then? She made some bright, empty remark and moved away.

"You're one of the Prior daughters, I presume?"

With an effort, Hilary wrenched her thoughts from Adam and Louise to look up at the tall, sandy-haired man with bushy eyebrows.

"Name's Tom Denton – previous owner of your house."

"Of course. How do you do?"

"All the better for seeing you, m'dear." He leered down at her and she realized sinkingly that he'd already had too much to drink. "You like the house? The bumps in the night don't worry you?"

"I don't think I understand."

He tapped the side of his nose significantly. "Had to keep quiet about it till the house was sold but we can admit it now, can't we?''

An apprehensive ripple zigzagged down Hilary's spine but before she could reply Geoff Silcox came to her rescue, taking Mr Denton's arm. "Come along, old chap, you were just about to regale us with your gliding experiences!" And with a wink over his shoulder at Hilary, he led him away.

The young people were sitting on the floor at the far end of the room. Hilary was amused to note that her brother's eyes were riveted on the prettier of the twins. He seemed to have revised his opinion of them. She wondered for a moment whether to go across and join them, but decided against it. They were all several years younger than she was and might feel inhibited by her presence. Perhaps after all it was a pity that Geoff had rescued her from Tom Denton. Provided she could avoid his beery breath, his conversation about Conningley might have proved interesting.

The men were standing in a group by the window while their wives sat together with their plates on their laps talking about old times. Rona was saying, "Do you remember the day my car broke down on the way to the tennis match and Marion stood as bold as brass at the side of the road and hitched a lift on a lorry?" She stopped, glanced round the circle of slightly embarrassed faces, and flushed.

"Poor Marion," Julia said quietly into the awkward silence. "She'll never be able to do that again."

Linda said in a low voice, "You've been to see her, I suppose?"

"Yes, and she's been to see us. In fact, she's coming again tomorrow."

"But I understood she never left the house?"

"She's open to persuasion," Julia replied. The rest of them exchanged glances and Moira Silcox said:

"I know what you must be thinking, Julia, that we turned out to be a pretty rotten lot of friends. But we did try at first, honestly, and nearly got our heads bitten off for our trouble."

"Yes, she said it was probably her own fault, but you know how she is."

"She discussed it with you? What else did she say?"

"That you all visited her in hospital but understandably didn't want the job for life, and that she'd probably have behaved the same way herself."

There was a brief silence. "I don't know about the rest of you," Tracy said at last, "but I'm prepared to try again. If Julia can make the effort to draw her out, so can I."

"You'll have to want to," Julia warned. "She doesn't take kindly to charity, but I know she'd love to see you." She hesitated. "Would it help to break the ice if you dropped in at Conningley some time when she's there?"

Hilary, who had been half listening to this exchange, helped herself to a cup of coffee and carried it through the open patio door. Outside, chairs had been arranged in groups and lights were strung from several of the trees. She sat down on a bench against the wall and stared unseeingly down the garden. The fact that she'd met Louise didn't alter anything. She'd known of her existence before. Perhaps it would have been wiser after all to have handed in the books impersonally at the shop, but that alternative was now lost to her. By the time the shop opened again on Monday she would be a member of the medical staff at Rokeby Hospital.

"Ah, there you are, young lady!" The slurred tones of Tom Denton. "Have to keep my eye on the prettiest girl at the party, you know! Your father's been telling me you're a doctor! You can take my pulse any day, and that's a promise!" He sat down beside her on the bench and fumbled for her hand but she manoeuvred the coffee cup with practised ease.

"Tell me," she said, partly to distract him from his amorous advances, "what it is at Conningley that goes bump in the night?"

He looked at her with drunken consternation. "I never said that!"

"You did, you know."

"Well, if I did, I shouldn't have. Mary'll have my life!"

"But after all," Hilary said reasonably. "the sale's gone through now. It can't make any difference."

His face cleared. "Yes, that's true. Got a good price for it too – better than we expected, in the circumstances." He seemed to have forgotten it was her family who had bought it.

"What circumstances, Mr Denton?"

"Call me Tom, m'dear. Always like pretty girls to call me Tom! Sounds so much more friendly!"

"You were telling me about the bumps." Hilary carefully removed his hand from her knee.

His face changed. "Frightened the life out of me, don't mind admitting it. Thought I'd had a drop too much, but Mary saw it too, not to mention Toby, poor little blighter. Thought he'd have a fit, the way he carried on."

"What was it that you saw?"

He glanced nervously over his shoulder. "You won't let Mary know I told you? Made me promise not to breathe a word, ever. Said people would think we were mad. Might well have been, too, if we'd stayed in that house much longer."

Hilary changed her tactics slightly. "But what did it look like?"

"About three feet high and covered in hair. That was bad enough, in all conscience, but what really put the wind up me was the impression it gave of being so unbelievably *old*. You know that phrase 'the Ancient of Days'? Well, that's how it was. You felt it should have died thousands of years ago." He gave a snort. "Perhaps it did!"

Hilary's hand was clamped on her saucer. The elemental, exactly as Clarissa Henry had described it.

"What's more," Tom Denton added, "the same night they found a dog up by that standing stone on the hill. Its throat had been torn out. Well now, we couldn't risk that happening to our little chap, could we?"

Oh Adam! Hilary thought suddenly, I do wish you were here!

Eleven

Marion said, "And how were my dear ex-friends?"

"Conscience-stricken! They've all resolved to turn over a new leaf."

"Oh Julia, you didn't appeal to their better natures, did you? I told you I –"

"No I didn't – or at least, only indirectly. Anyway, they needed jolting out of their ruts. They're just rather apprehensive about your reaction."

"They needn't be. You've mellowed me already, in the short time you've been back. Anyway, I can't afford to turn away any offers of friendship, can I? Who was there last night?"

"The usual crowd: Tracy and Paul, Kevin and Rona, Moira and Geoff – all complete with offspring, of course. And as a bonus, Tracy's young sister and the couple we bought this house from. The man works with Mike, apparently."

"What are they like?"

Julia smiled. "I can't say I was unduly impressed. The wife behaved very oddly, I thought, and her husband distinguished himself by drinking too much and making a pass at Hilary!"

"Well, he can hardly be blamed for that! And what about all the children? Have they changed much?"

"You should ask Nick that; it's my guess he's lost his heart to one of the despised twins! He couldn't stand them when he was younger, but I must admit they've grown into pretty girls and Amanda was stringing him along very deftly."

"He's a good-looking boy, your Nick – or will be, when he's outgrown this present gaucheness. He'll break a few hearts in his time, I don't doubt – possibly poor little Amanda's for a start!" She turned to Hilary, who had been sitting silently beside them.

"And how about you, Madam? All set to start work tomorrow?"

"Just about, yes."

"Looking forward to it?"

"Yes, I am. It's been quite a long break since Finals."

"And I suppose you're at a bit of a loose end, with that young man of yours so far away."

Hilary's eyes dropped. "Yes."

Brian meanwhile was pacing up and down the terrace, watched a little uneasily by Gavin.

"What is it, old man? Why don't you sit down and take the load off your feet? I'll be opening the bar in a moment or two." He noticed that Brian's face looked rather gaunt and there were two bright spots of colour on his cheeks.

"I've been sitting down all morning. What I need is a bit of exercise." Unable to hold back the query any longer, he said abruptly, "Where's Van?"

"Vanessa?" Her father looked bewildered. "I don't know, but she'll be back in time for lunch, wherever she is, you can rely on that!"

"I think if you'll excuse me I'll just go for a short stroll up the hill. I shan't be long."

"Up the hill?" Gaving stared at him. "What the hell for?"

"As I said, just a spot of exercise – to work up an appetite for lunch!"

Before Gavin could try to dissuade him he swung away over the grass and started striding up the slope. With a helpless shrug of his shoulders Gavin went into the house.

Brian saw Vanessa the moment he came over the brow of

the hill, and the feverish excitement which had propelled
him to go in search of her rose like a tide inside him. She
was sitting on the altar slab of the Stone with her hands
clasped in her lap and round her neck hung the rather
clumsy stone she had worn when she came to his bedroom.
He went slowly towards her, and the eyes she turned to him
were the all-powerful, all-knowing ones which had haunted
him. As he reached her he instinctively dropped to his knees
and lifted her hand to his lips. There seemed nothing
incongruous about his action and she sat impassively,
accepting the tribute. Then she reached forward and gently
pulled his head down on to her lap, her fingers moving
slowly, searchingly, over his face and hair.

"Bran," she murmured softly, "Bran the Blessed and his
wondrous Head!"

He stumbled to his feet and reached for her convulsively
but something in her gaze stopped him.

"You no longer fear the Stone," she said in that vibrant
tone he remembered so well.

For the first time since he'd reached it he remembered
the suffocating panic which had engulfed him on his
previous visit. "No," he said wonderingly, "No, I don't"

"Then all is well. Its sovereignty is complete. You accept
that? Total subjection of mind and body?"

"I – I don't –"

She smiled, more an involuntary tightening of the muscles
than an expression of pleasure. "The physical test I believe
you remember."

His whole body seemed to burn and he nodded without
speaking.

"The mental one was equally successful." And as he
looked at her uncomprehendingly, she added, "It was I
who called you out into the storm. You obeyed me without
question."

Ideas, realizations, clattered laboriously round his head
and he fumbled clumsily after them. He'd been thinking of
her, certainly, before he went rushing out into the rain-

filled darkness. Or was it the Stone which had been in his mind? Perhaps in some strange way they were one and the same.

"I ask you again," she said softly, "Do you accept its sovereignty?"

He felt every nerve quiver in his body. "I do."

"And you will continue to submit to it until the end?"

"Until the end," he repeated, and it was like a troth.

Slowly she raised her arms to remove the stone pendant and slipped it into her pocket. A shutter seemed to flicker at the back of her eyes and she said haltingly, "Hello, Uncle Bran! How long have you been here? I must have fallen asleep."

He stared at her painfully, the abrupt transition too sudden for him to adjust. "I suppose your watch has stopped," he said flatly.

"Oh yes. I don't even bother to look at it now, when I'm up here." Something in the hungry intensity of his gaze disturbed her and she asked uncertainly, "Is anything wrong?"

"How can you ask me that?" he said in a low voice. "You must know how –"

But of course she didn't. This was his own Vanessa from the old days, the child who had happily joined him for tea last week. He had thought then he could come to terms with the aberration, not realizing that the Other would return and set his senses reeling again.

"We'd better go back for lunch," he said woodenly. She held out a hand for him to help her down from the slab and he caught hold of it convulsively, not letting go of it as they started to walk side by side down the hill. He felt her glance curiously at him but kept his eyes on the ground at his feet, and in silence they returned to the garden and the rest of the family. They were all staring at him but he did not care. With Vanessa beside him he could face the entire world.

"Gavin, whatever's wrong with Brian?" Julia turned from

waving the Cresswells' car away to face her husband.

"God knows. He was certainly behaving very strangely. Did Marion say anything?"

"Only that he'd been 'off-colour', as she put it, since the golf club dinner."

"That's over a week ago now. It couldn't have been anything there that upset him, surely. Anyway, the trouble seems to be more – mental. He's living on his nerves."

Hilary came out of the front door behind them, some books in her hand. Gavin put an arm round her. "How did Brian's behaviour strike you, Doctor?"

"He seems to be under a strain, certainly. Perhaps he and Marion have had a row. You know how controlled he always is. He's been bottling things up for a long time now and if he did let fly at her, he'd have a fantastic guilt complex about it." She glanced at their anxious faces. "I shouldn't worry too much, it'll all blow over. I'm just going to return some books I borrowed. I shan't be very long."

"All right, dear." Still abstracted, they turned back to the house, and with her heart beating rather more strongly than the occasion warranted, Hilary went on down the drive in search of Adam. She had looked up his home address in the telephone directory. It was farther along the main road, beyond the road which led to the gliding club.

She went firmly up the path and rang the bell. The door was opened by a pretty woman in her fifties, who looked at her enquiringly.

"Good afternoon. I wonder if I could have a word with Adam, please? I've brought back some papers he lent me."

"Yes. Yes, of course." Joy Sandys recollected her manners and stood to one side. "Do come in. I think he's up in his room." She showed Hilary into the sitting-room and went to the foot of the stairs.

"Adam?"

"Hello?"

"Could you come down for a moment, please?" Deliberately she refrained from saying he had a visitor, intrigued to see his reaction. And she was not disappointed.

He came into the room fastening his watch strap. "Yes? What –" And then, caught completely off guard, "Hilary!" Well satisfied, his mother withdrew, closing the door softly behind her.

"I've brought your books back," Hilary said quietly.

"Thanks." He was trying to adjust to the pleasure her appearance had given him. He hadn't expected to see her again for some time. "What are your conclusions, now you've had a chance to study them?"

"You were right, they're decidedly unnerving – the diary especially."

He smiled slightly. "You've revised your opinion on the benefits of folklore and legend?"

She flushed. "I must have sounded terribly patronizing. I'm sorry."

"Of course you didn't. Look, you don't have to rush away, do you? Can I get you a drink?"

"Thanks – something long and cold."

She waited until he had poured the drinks and was handing her a glass before she said casually, "I met your friend Louise last night."

He looked up quickly. "Really? Where was that?"

"At a party, in Haddenham."

"What exciting lives you lead! I didn't know you had mutual friends."

"We knew the Pembrooks when we lived there and Louise went along with her sister. I hadn't realized you'd discussed the diary with her."

"You don't mind, do you?"

"No, I was surprised, that's all. She asked if I was going to tell Vanessa about it."

"And are you?" He motioned her to the sofa and sat down beside her.

"I don't know. I've no idea how she'd react." She stared down into her glass. "When I'd read through it all I decided I'd better go and have a look at the Stone myself."

"And how did it strike you?"

"If I hadn't heard about it, I shouldn't have given it a second thought."

"No vibes at all?"

"Positively none. I even ran my fingers round that little depression. There was the remains of something sticky inside which smelled like milk but that's hardly plausible, surely?"

"It could well be, as a matter of fact. Milk used to be poured in as a substitute for blood. Perhaps it still is."

She caught her breath. "Anyway, the thing that interested me most was the very well-worn track which leads from our gate up to the Stone. On the way back I discovered it didn't start at the gate as I'd thought but came all the way up from the main road. I followed it down and it ended at Mrs Hare's cottage."

"Well, well, well!" Adam said softly. "The lady with the milk, no doubt. I told you we were bedevilled by hares!"

"There's something else," she said in a low voice. "The people who lived in the house before us were also at the party last night. The husband was rather tight and he told me the reason they moved was because they saw the – the Elemental. It actually came down to the house." Her voice shook and Adam's hand went swiftly over hers, gripping it reassuringly. She drew a deep breath. "Sorry. I haven't been able to stop thinking about it."

"Can you tell me exactly what he said?"

Stumblingly she repeated Tom Denton's words about his wife and the dog also seeing the creature and his description of it.

"I shouldn't place too much importance on it," Adam said slowly. "He was probably only trying to frighten you."

"I don't think so. He was frightened himself."

"Well, if he was tight last night he might make a habit of being. Perhaps it was just a variation on the ubiquitous pink elephant!"

"But it fitted so exactly with Clarissa's description."

"He could have read somewhere about the Guardian of the Stone, even seen an illustration of it, and subconsciously projected the image into his drunken stupor or whatever."

After a moment she said quietly, "Yes, of course. I'm being very silly."

"You're not being silly at all," he said gently. "There's something invidious about these ancient superstitions that can reach out and close over your mind. That's what happened to Clarissa, after all. It makes you realize that our so-called civilization is only a very thin veneer spread over thousands of years of primitive beliefs and fears. All we can do is try to keep a sense of proportion."

"I suppose so. It serves me right for being so sceptical the other evening. Thanks for calming me down, Adam. I'm glad I came."

"So am I." He became aware that his hand was still on hers and removed it as inconspicuously as possible. She smiled a little shakily.

"I was almost on the point of trying to turn the family out of the house! Do you think that's really why the Dentons left?"

"I very much doubt it. They probably discovered dry rot somewhere and didn't want to be lumbered with the bill!"

"What is an elemental, though? Is there any basis for belief in it?"

He shrugged. "No more than for any other mythical creature, I suppose. 'Here be dragons', and so on. They were generally regarded as Guardians of the Stone or Barrow they inhabited."

"A few thousand years ago," she said slowly, "these hills and valleys were riddled with Celtic gods, some human, some animal, some a mixture of both. We still have the remains of their temples all around us – stone circles, henges, hill-forts. Perhaps it's just remotely possible that one or two of the gods themselves have survived as well."

"I thought you were going to stop being fanciful."

"Yes, I am. I promise." She drained her glass. "I'd better

be going. I've still my packing to finish."

"I'll walk back with you."

There was no-one in the hall and they went in silence out of the house and along the main road. On the far side of it was the gate through which they had gone to the Green Man, and Hilary found herself wishing after all that she wasn't starting work tomorrow and could look forward to walking that way with Adam again. But it would not do to see too much of Adam Sandys. After all, he had Louise. At the gateway of Conningley they stopped and looked at each other a little self-consciously.

"No more worries about ghosties and ghoulies?"

"No."

"I hope all goes well at the hospital."

"Thanks. It'll certainly be hard work. Six months' medicine, to start off with."

"Rather you than me. When will you be back?"

"I don't know yet."

"Well good-bye again. Take care."

She nodded and he moved suddenly, pulling her towards him and kissing her hard on the mouth. He was half-way round the crescent before she'd recovered her breath. With her heart rioting inside her she went slowly up the drive to the house.

His mother was in the hall when he got back and he resigned himself to the inevitable inquisition. It began at once.

"Who was that perfectly gorgeous girl, Adam? You might have introduced her to me!"

"You were so busy being discreet I didn't have the chance. Her name is Hilary Prior."

"You've kept her pretty well hidden."

"It wasn't difficult. I hardly know her."

Incredibly it was true, but his mother gave a disbelieving laugh. "My dear Adam, I'm not a fool! I've been waiting for ten years to see an expression like that on your face!"

"I'm afraid you're rather off-beam," he said shortly.

"She happens to be engaged to someone out in Africa."

Her eyes softened. "I see." She put a hand on his arm. "Darling. I'm sorry. Does she know how you feel?"

"I doubt it, since I don't myself." He hesitated. "Mother, I'd be grateful if you didn't mention her in front of Father or David. They'd only get the wrong impression and in any case she starts work at Rokeby Hospital tomorrow. In all probability I shan't see her again." His eyes fell from hers. "Let me know when supper's ready, will you? I'll be in my room."

He went past her up the stairs and she stood looking after him, aching to comfort him. For however he might try to disguise the fact, to her and to himself, she knew that girl with her wide, vulnerable mouth and honey-coloured hair meant more to him than any of the others he had known.

Her bed felt cool and fresh. Marion settled back and closed her eyes. Julia was right: it did her good to go out occasionally, exhausting though it was. It made her feel less of an outcast, more involved with the old, everyday world she'd seen so little of over the past three years.

"Is there anything I can get you?" Brian's voice was jerky, dragging her back from her pleasantly dozing reflections.

"Not for the moment, thank you." She studied his face critically. It was flushed, with dark circles under the eyes. "Brian, what is it? What's worrying you?"

He looked down at her quickly. "Nothing."

"You've been behaving most peculiarly. I'm sure the Priors noticed it. Can't you tell me what's wrong?"

He ran his fingers through his hair. "Nothing's wrong, Marion. Really."

She lay watching him, surprising in herself a forgotten tenderness. She did not give him an easy life and when he tried to please her, more often than not she snapped at him. Perhaps she ought to make him feel she needed him more. She said slowly, "If you've nothing in particular to do, I know what I should like."

"What's that?"

"Would you read to me for a while? One of my old favourites – Jane Austen, perhaps."

"Yes. Yes, of course."

It was very soothing to lie back with her eyes closed and let the well-remembered words flow into her brain. Brian read well and his voice was one of the first things about him that had attracted her. But this evening he did not seem to be concentrating. Several times he stumbled over a word, repeated himself, lost his place. She made no comment but turned her head to watch him and with a sense of shocked disbelief saw that his eyes were full of tears. Never in twenty years of marriage had she seen such a thing.

"Brian –" Her voice broke into his halting words and he stopped dead. "Please, my dear, let me help. Don't shut me out."

His face crumpled at her unexpected gentleness and, dropping the book, he slid to his knees beside the bed, burying his face in the blanket while great tearing sobs shook his body. Marion stared at him, appalled, completely at a loss how to deal with this breakdown. Inch by painful inch she moved her hand until she could at least lay it against his tear-wet face, and as her mind searched frantically for some reason for his distress, she believed that she had found it.

She said carefully. "You've met someone else, haven't you? That's what's troubling you. Tell me about it. I'll understand."

His voice was muffled and she could only distinguish the words, "Oh God! Oh God!"

"I don't mind, you know," she went on gently. "I've been expecting this for the last three years. You've been wonderful to me, Brian. Don't think, just because I'm so bitchy, that I don't appreciate it. But you have a right to a life of your own. There's no reason why your future should be permanently blighted."

He shook his head violently. "You don't understand. How could you? I don't myself."

"Do you love someone? Is that it?"

He was suddenly still, seemed almost to have stopped breathing. She moved her fingers against his face. "It doesn't matter – really. You're quite free to go."

He lifted his head and she stared with compassion into his ravaged face. "Free?" he echoed harshly. "I shall never be free again!"

"Then go to her. You have my blessing, truly."

He stared at her as though he didn't understand what she was saying, but her words must in some distorted way have reached him, for he exclaimed, "How can I go to a spirit five thousand years in the past?"

Marion stared blankly at him, the first real fear moving inside her. The breakdown must be much more serious than she'd imagined. What did one do in such circumstances? If only she wasn't so helpless, lying here like a vegetable unable to summon help! It was Miss Fergusson's evening off but Daisy would be down in the kitchen. Could she phone a doctor? But how to explain, without distressing Brian still further?

"Tell me about her," she said jerkily, playing for time.

He was still staring at her but his eyes took on a glazed, in-looking expression. "She is wonderful and relentless and cruel. She knows everything and demands everything. And sometimes –" his face contorted again – "she's only fifteen years old!"

The focus of his gaze shifted suddenly and he saw her again, read perhaps the fear on her face, because quite suddenly he was completely calm.

"Marion, I'm sorry." He spoke in his normal voice, only a slight breathlessness reminiscent of the recent paroxysm. "I'd no right to frighten you like that, it was unforgivable. I've been under a strain for some time and suddenly everything snapped. I'll go and have a wash and then we'll finish the chapter."

And as she gazed up at him in overwhelming relief he bent and gently kissed her forehead. As he went from the room, her own eyes were full of tears.

Julia tapped on the door and put her head round. "All right, darling? Everything packed?"

Hilary was sitting at her desk and the half-open case, piled high with books and clothes, was on the floor.

"Yes, thanks." She hesitated. "I've just been writing to Chris."

Julia waited, sensing there was more to come, and after a moment, not looking at her, Hilary said quietly, "I've told him I want to break off the engagement."

Julia came fully into the room, closed the door behind her and sat down on the end of the bed. "I have to admit I'm not too surprised. What made you decide?"

"It's been building up for months. The magic had gone out of it even before he went away and his letters have increased the gulf rather than bridging it. He just – doesn't light sparks in me any more."

"You don't think it might be wiser to let things run on until he comes home? Being apart is bound to be a strain. You might change your mind when you see him again."

"No. It was wonderful while it lasted, but it's over now. I think he realizes it too."

Julia said carefully, "You saw Adam Sandys again this evening, didn't you?"

"Don't try to be subtle, Mother! This has nothing to do with Adam. Anyway, he has a girl friend of his own – Tracy Turner's sister."

"The girl at the Pembrooks'? I didn't know that." She studied her daughter's face. "You do like him though, don't you?"

"Yes I like him, but I hardly know him." Unconsciously she was repeating Adam's own defence. "Meeting him certainly hasn't influenced my decision, if that's what you're wondering."

Julia stood up. "All right, darling, you know best, of course. But it seems a shame. Perhaps the real mistake was in getting engaged at all. You're not too upset about it, are you?"

"Not really, especially as I think it will come as a relief to Chris too. I felt it was best to do it now, so I can start work tomorrow with a clean slate." She smiled a little. "Don't worry, I shan't cry myself to sleep!"

Julia bent to kiss her. "See you in the morning, then. I'll give you a call at seven. Your days of leisurely rising are at an end, Doctor!"

But as Hilary reached up to switch off her light her mind was neither on the ring she had put away in a drawer nor her forthcoming departure for the hospital. She was remembering Adam's hand over hers and the unexpected abruptness of his kiss. And unwillingly she thought of Louise with her large grey eyes and recalled Rona's casual enquiry: "How's that dishy young man of yours?"

With an impatient sigh she turned on her side, pulled the sheet over her head and went to sleep.

Twelve

Nick lay flat on his back squinting up into the sky at the great, dipping shape of the glider.

"Do you think she'd come?" he asked, chewing on a blade of grass.

"Dunno. She might, if she fancies you."

"We'd need to include her sister. They do everything together."

"Everything?" Steve raised an eyebrow. "Could be limiting!"

Nick grinned and didn't reply. After a moment he said, "You'd like Claire."

"I see. So I'm to be lumbered with the sister."

"It's not a question of being lumbered; she's a nice girl. Not as bouncy as Amanda but great fun and quite pretty."

"And what about this Bruce bloke Amanda was with the other evening?"

"He's a drip. You needn't worry about him."

"But if he's taking her out —"

"I don't think he is. She was playing up to him to spite me."

"Big head!" said Steve affably.

"Well, Claire hinted as much. Anyway, she can only say 'no'."

Steve rolled over on his stomach. "You're quite keen, aren't you?"

"It's not that, it's just that we were always moaning about the lack of girls round here, and now I've found us a couple." He paused. "What is a 'hop', exactly?"

"I shouldn't think it'll be much like a disco. Most of the people up there are a lot older than us. There'll probably be foxtrots and things like that."

Nick looked alarmed. "Do you think so? Well, I suppose we could always sit and talk in the bar."

"That could be expensive. Do they drink much?"

"They didn't on Saturday." Another pause. "Shall I give her a ring, then?"

"Might as well."

Nick closed his eyes against the glare of the sky and let his thoughts circle idly round Amanda — as, in fact, they'd done continually since Saturday. The dance wasn't for another ten days, though. When he phoned to invite her, he could suggest meeting before that — tomorrow, for instance. No point in wasting time. If she agreed to go out with him there were all kinds of things they could do — picnics, bike rides — he might even interest her in gliding. Pretty, vivacious Amanda. The summer stretched in front of him, suddenly full of promise. Over two months before he need start thinking about University. A lot could happen in two months.

Marion said abruptly, "I felt I just had to speak to you. I'm extremely worried about Brian."

Julia sat down slowly on the bed, cradling the telephone under her chin while she reached for a cigarette. "In what way?" she hedged.

"Didn't his behaviour yesterday strike you as – unusual?"

"Yes it did, actually. Gavin and I were talking about it after you'd gone. Has he been overworking, do you think?"

"Not more than usual. This all came on relatively suddenly a couple of weeks ago. It's all the more worrying because I was hoping that now you're back he would relax a little and enjoy a bit more social life. But if anything he seems worse when we're with you than he does at home. Perhaps it's the contrast, between your way of life and ours."

"Probably there's some problem at work which is worrying him. I'm sure it'll pass if you play it down."

"That's what I was telling myself, until last night. Julia –" The disbelief was still in her voice. "He broke down and cried! It was absolutely shattering and I felt so *useless*, just having to lie there. And he was rambling something about five-thousand-year-old spirits!"

Julia frowned down at the carpet. "In that case I should say he ought to see a doctor."

"But he won't! I suggested it this morning but he insists there's nothing wrong with him. I wish I could believe that! The odd thing is that he changes so quickly. Last night he recovered completely within a few minutes and calmly went on reading *Persuasion*."

"Perhaps the tears provided the relief he needed. I'm so sorry, Marion, it must be worrying for you. Tell you what: we'll have him over for a meal like you asked. I hadn't forgotten but this last week I've been helping Hilary sort out her things for Rokeby and didn't get round to it. Then, if he still seems to be under a strain, Gavin can have a word with him and see if he can get to the bottom of it."

"Would he? I'd be so grateful."

"In fact, they could probably meet for lunch even before that, and fix a convenient evening then. The decorators are starting on the dining-room tomorrow but I don't suppose he'll mind eating in the kitchen." She paused. "Might he be drinking more than usual?"

"I thought so at first, after that dinner he went to with Gavin, but now I'm not so sure. Not that I've any way of proving it, one way or the other. I can hardly ask Miss Fergusson to mark the whisky bottle. He's certainly very jittery and absent-minded and sometimes he – he does peculiar things." She hesitated. "I wasn't going to mention this, but perhaps it'll give you some idea of what I'm up against. You remember that storm we had last week? The next morning Daisy found a pair of Brian's pyjamas on the bathroom floor. They were soaking wet and there was mud round the bottom of the trousers. Julia, he must have been in the garden, and presumably without even a mac! Now why the hell should he go into the garden in the middle of the night in a thunderstorm?"

It was a rhetorical question and Julia didn't attempt a reply. Things were obviously much more serious than she'd realized. Poor Brian, he'd always been so calm and practical, so completely in control of himself. Perhaps, as Hilary said, he had been bottling things up for too long.

"Have I done this to him, Julia? Because if I have I'll never forgive myself. We stopped loving each other years ago, but we certainly never set out to hurt one another. I told him before I shouldn't stand in his way if he wanted to leave me, and I said so again last night. I thought perhaps from the way he was carrying on that he'd fallen for someone else and was smitten by guilt. But he needn't be. It may sound callous, but I could manage perfectly well without him. I don't mean that unkindly, but after all I have Daisy and the Scottish dragon and as you know Daddy left me very well provided for. I'd much rather he went than feel he was staying against his will, out of a sense of duty."

"I know," Julia said awkwardly. "Try not to worry, Marion. I'll get Gavin to have a word with him so leave it with us now and I'll let you know how we get on."

But when, two days later, Brian came for dinner, he seemed completely himself. From behind his chair Gavin raised his eyebrows at Julia and gave a little shrug. There appeared to be no cause for concern whatever and Julia relaxed, comforting herself with the thought that as she'd predicted whatever had been worrying him must have sorted itself out.

The decorators had effectively barred them from the dining-room, and the meal in the kitchen, with all the windows open to the garden, had an informal *al fresco* air, accentuated by the fact that Julia had provided chicken in a basket and the easiest way to eat it was in their fingers.

"I wonder what Hilary's having for dinner," Vanessa remarked with sisterly sympathy, gnawing on a bone.

"They probably feed their staff better than the patients!" Brian rejoined. "They'd have to, to keep their strength up during those long working hours. When is she likely to have some free time?"

"In a couple of weeks, we hope. Did Gavin tell you he went along with her to buy a second-hand car? With independent transport she can be home in fifteen minutes but while she's working from eight in the morning till midnight there doesn't seem much point."

Brian whistled. "And I consider my hours are too long!"

"They probably are," Gavin put in, mindful of his instructions. "I keep telling you to relax more and take up some outside interest."

Nick passed his plate down the table for a second helping. "I've been meaning to ask you, Brian – are you interested in gliding?"

"Oh Nick really!" groaned his father. "Have you no other topic of conversation?"

"He has with Steve!" Vanessa said wickedly. "Amanda Pembrook!"

Nick reddened. "I've told you before about listening to other people's conversations."

"And I've told you before that I've no option if you will hold long post-mortems on the phone. 'I said to her' and 'she said to me' – it sounded like a game of consequences!"

"I asked about the gliding," Nick resumed with dignity, "because I saw you up there the other evening."

As Gavin glanced at him in surprise, Brian said quickly, "Not me, old fellow."

"But I'm sure it was! I almost called out to you!"

"Just as well you didn't, then."

"Over by the winch," Nick pursued. "In the direction of the Stone."

Brian looked across at him. "If you're asking me to produce an alibi," he said mildly, "I'm afraid I can't. You'll just have to take my word for it that I wasn't there."

"Let it drop, Nick, for heaven's sake!" Julia put in. "What does it matter, anyway?"

There was a moment's rather awkward silence and then Vanessa, who appeared not to have been listening to the exchange, said suddenly, "I've just thought: aren't we going to have a holiday this year?"

"The whole summer's a holiday for you!" Julia said with a smile, glad of the change of subject.

"I mean as a family."

"Can't afford it," Gavin said firmly. "Moving house put paid to that for this year."

"But even if we can't go abroad, surely we could at least go down to Devon or Cornwall? Think of those lovely cream teas!"

Nick, still smarting from her teasing, said acidly, "Van judges everywhere by its food content! Golden beaches – surf – fantastic scenery – nix! What can you get to eat?"

Brian said with a laugh, "Well, you don't have to go as far as Devon if all you want is a cream tea. There's a little place the other side of Tring that serves them. I'll take you if you like!"

"Will you, Uncle? That'd be lovely! When?"

"You won't be allowed to forget it," Gavin warned him.

"I don't want to but I'm afraid I'll have to look in my diary before I can make a definite date. I'll phone and let you know, Van."

The meal over, Gavin and Brian carried their coffee out to the terrace and Nick went through to the sitting-room to watch television. Vanessa glanced at her mother.

"I get the impression we're not supposed to join them out there."

"Very astute of you, darling. Daddy wants a word in private with Brian. You can help me with the dishes."

Vanessa pulled a face and began to clear the table. "He seems all right today, doesn't he?"

Julia glanced at her quickly. "Yes, he does. We were probably worrying unnecessarily."

Out on the terrace, Brian turned to Gavin with a smile. "O.K., I'm ready. Shoot!"

"How do you mean?"

"Oh, come on! We all know you've been deputed to have a serious chat with me. You were skirting round it at lunch yesterday so let's get it over."

"It doesn't seem necessary any more. I just felt you were under a strain and wondered if I could be of help."

"Did Marion put you up to it? I'm afraid I made rather an exhibition of myself the other evening."

"Things can get on top of you at times. It happens to everyone. All the same, it might be an idea to have a complete check-up. I'm thinking along the same lines myself. The late forties are a notorious time for heart attacks and such."

"I doubt if I'm a candidate for one. I'm not overweight, I don't smoke and – golf club dinners apart! – I only drink in moderation."

"But you don't get much exercise, do you?"

"I spend most evenings running up and down stairs," Brian returned a little grimly. "I don't know what else you'd call that."

"Have you thought any more about joining the golf club? I'd be happy to propose you."

"It's very good of you, but there's no urgency. I'm sorry if I've put the wind up everyone but I assure you there's nothing wrong with me."

"But you'll think seriously about a check-up?"

"I might, if I feel run down again."

And with that Gavin had to be content.

Adam saw Vanessa as he came out of the antique shop and felt a momentary apprehension. He had still not formulated any excuse for not handing back the diary but he was reluctant to do so and knew Hilary shared his misgivings. He contemplated dodging back into the doorway, but was too late. She turned and saw him and her face lit up in a smile.

"I was just wondering whether to treat myself to an éclair!" she greeted him, indicating the bakery window which had been engaging her attention.

"At ten o'clock in the morning?"

"Why not?" She glanced at the glossy brochure in his hand. "I think Mummy will be in to see you soon. She's having the dining-room painted and has decided she wants new chairs as well. New old chairs, that is!"

Adam found he was watching her face for any likeness to Hilary but any that there was was only momentary, a passing expression, and anyway he was not going to think about Hilary. He would have liked to ask her whether she had finished with the spell-stones yet, but any mention of them would inevitably remind her about the diary and he regretfully refrained. However, meeting her had reminded him that he had not yet returned the magazine to Louise, and since he had to go into Aylesbury later that morning he resolved to do so.

He had been slightly apprehensive about this first meeting after the ending of their affair, but to his relief Louise appeared perfectly natural.

"Don't rush off, Adam, I've been wanting to talk to you about that diary. I've been trying to trace the family for permission to print it, but they seem to have disappeared without trace. It would be difficult to prove ownership. I suppose the Priors have as much right as anyone."

"Probably." He perched thoughtfully on her desk. "If I were you, though, I shouldn't rush into print just yet. Give it a month or two, so Vanessa can get over the initial impact."

She looked up at him shrewdly. "Is that the real reason, or do you think there's more to come?"

He smiled a little shamefacedly. "Well, we're just coming up to the hundred year mark and events do seem to be – what's the 'in' word? – escalating up there. You might well get a better story by holding your hand till at least the end of the year."

"You don't really believe all that rubbish, do you?" she demanded incredulously.

"Not with my rational mind, of course, but subconsciously I'm not quite so sure. Don't forget my family has been around that area for centuries. The legend's bred into us, even if we never talk about it." He laughed at her sceptical face and stood up. "Come on, I'll buy you lunch at the King's Head."

When they were seated in the bar with their snack lunch Louise said casually, "I suppose you heard that Hilary and I met at the Pembrooks'?"

"I did, yes."

She waited but he didn't elaborate and she went on, "What did you both decide, about Vanessa and the diary?"

"That we'd prefer to play it down. I'm certainly not anxious to give her the transcript, it's altogether too explicit. As a matter of fact I saw her in Ickfield this morning. I was desperately trying to think of an excuse for hanging on to it, but she never even mentioned the thing!"

"Perhaps she's forgotten about it."

"I wish I could believe that."

Louise looked at him consideringly for a moment. "Did you follow up any of those references in the article?"

"I did, and there was a positive *embaras de richesse*! Priests of the Stone and reincarnation, to mention but two."

"Ye gods! So it backed up what Clarissa Thing had written in her diary?"

"To a large extent, yes, but of course she might have had access to some of the stories herself. On the other hand, there does seem to be some historical evidence for these periodic outbreaks of violence."

"Which is why you advise me to sit on the story for a while?"

He smiled. "Let's just say I'm hedging my bet. We can't rule out the possibility that the legend has been responsible for the continuing violence, if people believed it sufficiently to give fate a nudge."

"In any event, the end result was the same."

"True. The Stone had its blood-bath and the superstitions died down until the next time."

Louise shuddered. "I'm glad I don't live in that creepy village of yours!"

"I'd sooner settle for violence once every hundred years than live in a city, where it happens every day. By the way, I've got the books in the back of the car, if you'd like to borrow them. I was going to drop them off at the library but they're not due back for another two weeks yet."

"Thanks. I'd like to see them, and the transcript of the diary too, if you could drop it in some time." She smiled suddenly. "It wasn't so bad after all, was it?"

"What wasn't?"

"Our first meeting on the new footing. You should have seen your face when you came into the office – a picture of apprehension!''

"Nonsense!" Adam gave a slightly uncomfortable laugh.

"You know I'm right, even if you won't admit it. But we were friends for quite a long time in the beginning, weren't we, before the other thing developed, and there's no reason why we can't be again. We were always able to relax with each other."

"Yes. Bless you, Louise." He put his hand briefly over hers. "Unfortunately, however, I mustn't relax any longer at the moment. I've a man coming to see me about a sideboard at two-thirty."

"And I've some copy to read through." She sighed and rose to her feet. "I'll walk back to the car with you and collect the books. I don't doubt they make fascinating reading, but I warn you I refuse point-blank to be brainwashed into believing them."

"So much for the open-minded Press!" said Adam with a laugh.

In her room at Conningley, Vanessa lay on her bed, her fingers absent-mindedly caressing the smooth shapes of the spell-stones – and in his Aylesbury office Brian felt a cool ripple pass over his skin. He looked up from his papers, recognizing the sensation without knowing precisely what had caused it. Some kind of telepathy, he thought vaguely, a signal passing to him from the force that contolled Vanessa. Today it was a weak signal, demanding no response from him other than an acknowledgement that the lines were still open between them.

Before he could prevent it his mind slipped back to Sunday, and the obeisance he had made before the Stone. The experience had affected him even more profoundly than he'd realized, causing his breakdown in front of Marion and making the rest of them fear for his reason. It had taken an almost superhuman effort to put their minds at rest again but at least the lesson had not been wasted. He'd resolved that those disturbing memories should only be indulged in when he was completely alone. As he was now.

Total subjection, her voice whispered in his head. It was ironic how easily he had succumbed, when he had been so sure of his control over mind and body. He knew now that the first cataclysmic approach had been simply to shock him into awareness and that having achieved its objective, no further intimacies would be countenanced between them. Should her hands again move gloatingly over face and hair he must simply steel himself to withstand their ritual caress, for the force, coldly measuring his potential, was unconcerned that the sensations it had arbitrarily aroused continued to gnaw at him with no means of gratification. Service and worship were all that were required of him, and to that end he had sworn his fealty.

Shakily Brian drew out his handkerchief and wiped his wet palms. It – she – to what or whom was he referring? To Spirit or Stone, or to Vanessa, possesed by both? He drew a long, shuddering breath, recalling his promise to take her for a cream tea which he had deliberately delayed implementing. Suppose the other one came in her place – what then? Alone in the car along those deserted country lanes, might she possibly relent of her harsh treatment of him?

His hand slammed open-palmed on the top of his desk, upsetting the tray of paper-clips and sending his pen skidding to the floor. What price his iron control now? he thought with caustic self-loathing. For wherever the strange spirit came from, the body it manipulated was Vanessa's, and therefore for ever beyond his reach.

Slowly he lowered his forehead to the cool polished wood and prayed in words he could not begin to formulate for deliverance from his torment.

In the cottage at the foot of the hill path, Gerda Hare stood staring resentfully at the glider which circled overhead. It was almost dusk and still the pesky things kept floating past, delaying her pilgrimage to the Stone. It was becoming increasingly difficult to persuade Sam of her liking for these long solitary outings in the twilight and the boy Ben was looking at her these days with increasing suspicion. Still, she would not be troubling either of them much longer. Her mission was almost accomplished.

From the cupboard beneath the sink she took the small crock she used to carry the milk, and as always her hands began to tremble. The thick yellow milk splashed heavily into the earthenware jug and she covered it as she always did with a small piece of muslin. The glider had disappeared over the rim of the hill. Surely that would be the last one for tonight.

She listened for a moment to the strident sounds of a gun battle seeping through the wall from the television in the front room, where husband and step-son sat enthralled. If her luck held, she would be back before they even registered her absence. Tongue between lips, she let herself quietly out of the back door and across the small neat garden to the gate in the wall. Behind her as she began to climb, cars raced along the main road, their headlights cleaving bright tunnels out of the approaching darkness. She distrusted all modern machines – cars invading the village, planes the sky. How much more peaceful it used to be –

Her small feet went unerringly into the shadow of the trees, never straying from the beaten-down path they had trod so many times before. Over her head an owl hooted suddenly and she smiled a brief acknowledgement to Blodeuwedd, wife of the god Lleu. On her left the garden walls of Conningley loomed in the darkness and a strange tenderness came into her eyes as she thought of Vanessa. This one was more stable than Miss Clarissa. This time there would be no embarrassing accusations.

She saw the glow in the sky before she topped the rise, and the breath caught in her throat. It couldn't be reflected from the planes; their lights were red and green, not this soft mother-of-pearl. Then she saw it, the Druid Stone bathed in unearthly radiance, pulsing and throbbing in the warm night and beyond it the deserted hulk of the gliding club winch. Had they noticed it, the men who had been here so recently, or was this luminescence visible to her alone?

She hurried forward and reverently tipped the contents of the little jug into the hollow. As the cool liquid struck the stone there was a faint hissing sound before it seeped rapidly away. When it had all gone, Gerda stretched her body on the altar, forehead resting on the warm vibrating surface as an ecstatic radiance flooded through her. Time shivered into fragments and winds from other dimensions blew across her prostrate body, lifting the sparse hair and caressing the bony shoulders of this their acolyte. After a while she tremblingly raised herself and began the ritualistic circling on unsteady legs, three times in the direction of the sun, three times against the sun and three more sunward, reciting as she went a rhythmic almost mindless incantation to the gods: 'Aine, Cernunnos, Vitiris, Tiu, Ancasta, Andarta, Andraste, Don –'

A low humming was rising from the Stone and she knew she could not hold it in check much longer. The offering of milk was becoming a useless placebo; tomorrow she must bring a rabbit or chicken, but it would be necessary to remove the lifeless body before sunrise. There was talk enough in the village already.

She came to a halt, the ceremony completed, and as she stood there the glow began to fade from the Stone, at first almost imperceptibly then with increasing swiftness until it had merged back into seeming lifelessness and she stood alone in the almost-dark.

"Two weeks at most," she promised it silently. "Be patient – all will be fulfilled." And with a bow of her head, she took her leave of it and began the descent to her waiting family.

Thirteen

The weekend passed uneventfully. As Julia had arranged for Marion to spend the afternoon with her the following Tuesday, she did not invite the Cresswells on the Sunday and was guiltily aware of a sense of relief. Fond as she was of Marion, she was still not entirely comfortable in her company, and with Brian at the moment one couldn't be certain how he would behave. His seeming normality when he came to dinner had only partially reassured Julia; there had been a feverish glint in his eye which still disturbed her, though Gavin had been perfectly satisfied with the outcome of the evening.

"He's quite amenable to the idea of a check-up, but as he said there doesn't seem to be any urgency at the moment."

"There's something a little odd about him, though," Julia said slowly. "I can't describe it, but sometimes when he looks at Vanessa I can feel the hairs lift on the back of my neck."

"My darling girl, how primitive! Brian's always had a special feeling for Van, you know that."

"Yes, but it seems to have changed somehow. I know it sounds ludicrous, but I'm not altogether sure that I trust him any more."

"*Trust* him? For crying out loud! You're not ascribing Lolita tendencies to Brian of all people?"

"No, that's not quite what I meant. At least —" She frowned. "I don't know — he just *watches* her, all the time. Haven't you noticed? As though he's waiting for a sign of some sort."

"I'm beginning to think you're the one in need of a check-up! A sign, forsooth! Heaven spare me from over-imaginative mothers!"

So she let the subject drop, and as the days passed without Brian phoning to confirm about the cream tea she began to feel a little easier.

"Don't forget, Nick." she said at breakfast that Tuesday, "I want you to come with me after lunch to collect Marion. I can't manage her by myself but you needn't stay all afternoon. The Haddenham crowd will be dropping in, and Brian will collect her on his way home."

"Are you sure the two of you can cope?" Gavin asked anxiously.

"Oh yes. Miss Fergusson will help us get her into the car and we'll have her chair. I'm determined to play down the fuss as much as possible."

"For the benefit of Linda and co.?"

"Partly. There's no reason why Marion shouldn't visit them too, as long as she doesn't lose her confidence."

In the event it was Julia's own confidence that was lacking that afternoon, though she did her best to conceal the fact. The knowledge that she was, for the space of a few hours, totally responsible for Marion was suddenly overwhelming and she was inordinately grateful for Nick's young strength as he lifted her easily into her chair. Her reward came, though, when, established once more on the sitting-room sofa, Marion looked across at her and said wryly, "You've missed your vocation, do you know that? Such strength of will! I'd never had budged from home for anyone else!"

"But after this you will," Julia said rallyingly, "now that you realize how easy it is."

"Hm. Now tell me, am I supposed to look appropriately surprised when Linda and her mob just happen to drop in?"

"No, I realized that might be rather a strain! I told them I'd let you know they were coming."

"They're not going to subject me to any good works, are they?"

"I doubt it but I think they're sincerely sorry for neglecting you, so be a good girl and meet them halfway."

Vanessa glanced back towards the open french windows as she went up the garden. She'd promised her mother to put in an appearance some time during the afternoon, and obviously the best time would be while tea was being served. For the moment she wanted to visit the well. She'd been neglecting it lately in her absorption with the Stone, only passing it on her way to and from the gate, and this afternoon she intended to rectify the fault. She had a pail of water with her and a soft scrubbing brush and planned to clean up the ancient stonework and brush away the accumulated cobwebs. In the pocket of her jeans the spell-stones clicked companionably. She seldom went anywhere without them these days, since she couldn't be sure when the summons would come.

She frowned briefly, her thoughts confusing her as they so often did nowadays, implying a knowledge that was not really hers. She pushed her way through the brambles which were again beginning to encroach on the path and came into the clearing by the wall in the centre of which, dull under the cloudy sky, the well squatted like an immense toad.

Playing her usual game of 'Threes', Vanessa went round the well three times one way, three times the other, and three again for luck. Strange words were forming in her head: Aine, Cerunnos, Vitiris, Tiu – She stopped, put a hand on the rim of the well to ward off a sudden giddiness, and it was then, out of the corner of her eye, that she saw it. She froze, not turning her head, which she knew would startle it, but staring fixedly at the grass some inches to its left while Mrs Hare's words echoed in her memory: 'Its Guardian – a creature half-man, half-beast'. This then, this small crouching creature in the long grass, was what had scared the Dentons so much. If she turned her head quickly, would she see it, or would it simply prove to be a shadow flung by the outline of the well? But there was no sun today to cast shadows.

Very slowly, holding her breath, Vanessa turned her head and for a long minute, across unnumbered centuries, she and the Guardian of the Stone gazed unwinkingly at each other. It was so *old*! she thought wonderingly, unaccountably, unbelievably old, a relic of some long-forgotten Celtic religion still lingering in these timeless hills. Her eyes were smarting with the effort not to blink and when at last, rapidly, she did so, the creature disappeared instantly.

She bent down and laid her hand in the depression left by its body, but instead of the expected warmth an unnatural coldness chilled her, seeming to seep up from the dank earth far beneath. Straightening quickly, her hand went to her pocket, instinctively closing on the stones for protection, but to her surprise she discovered she was not after all afraid. Instead she was trying to memorize the features of the being she had seen so briefly: unwinking monkey-brown eyes as old as time, coarse hair falling over the low brow, broad barrel chest and long arms. Yet for all its primitive appearance, there had been undeniable intelligence there, at least part human and of quite incredible antiquity. An elemental – that's what Mrs Hare had called it. She had actually seen an elemental!

She dropped to her knees and almost sacrificially began to wash the sides of the well.

"Julia made us feel very ashamed," Linda was saying quietly. "I could so easily have invited you and Brian to the party. After all, you were an essential part of the old crowd."

"Spare yourself any concern on that score," Marion said forthrightly. "We wouldn't have come. Julia's working wonders as you see, but parties are still beyond me and in any case I'd have been a regular spectre at the feast, now wouldn't I?''

"But you'll come for tea at least, now we've broken the ice?''

"We'll see.''

Linda turned to Julia. "By the way, are you by any chance aware that we're being favoured with a considerable amount of your son's company?''

"Nick? How do you mean?''

"He appears to have taken quite a shine to Amanda. He and another boy are always on the doorstep!''

"And I thought he was spending his time at the gliding club! I hope they're not being a nuisance?''

"Far from it. They're keeping the twins occupied, which means I'm not having to drive them into Aylesbury every five minutes.''

"He's grown into a good-looking boy, hasn't he?'' Tracy put in. "And as for Hilary, she's a raving beauty! No wonder she's engaged!''

"As a matter of fact,'' Julia said quietly, "she isn't any more.''

"Oh no! What happened?''

"I think they just outgrew each other. As I said to Marion earlier, the mistake they made was trying to tie themselves down before Chris had his year abroad.''

"You can't blame the boy, though, for wanting to put a ring on her finger while he had the chance. He was probably afraid someone else would snap her up while he was away. Is she very upset about it?''

"Not unduly, I think. Her work's taking all her attention at the moment.''

"The traumas of parenthood!'' Moira said with a smile. "At least you haven't that to worry about, Marion!''

"No, I must say I've never regretted opting out, though poor Brian still gets broody from time to time, doesn't he, Julia?''

Julia looked at her quickly, remembering her recent

conversation with Gavin. "Yes, I suppose he does."

"He always did think the sun shone out of Vanessa. Where is she, by the way?"

"In the garden somewhere, I think. She'll be in soon, to see you."

Up by the well Vanessa sat back on her heels to survey her handiwork. The stonework was gleaming wetly and now that the grime of centuries had been removed she could distinguish curves and squirls cut into the stone in an intricate pattern. She stood up, stretched, and peered inside the well at the stagnant water far below. She would have liked to climb down and clean in there as well but she knew better than to attempt it on her own. Perhaps Nick would help her, if she could prise him away from that snooty Amanda Pembrook. In any case, it was time she went back to the house. Mrs Hare had been requested to stay on for an extra hour this afternoon to serve the tea. Her thoughts went to Marion, and from her to Brian, who would later come to collect her, and a quiver of excitement shook her as a picture of him filled her mind – or, more accurately, a picture of his head, with its thick brows and deeply set eyes, the strong shape of nose and mouth and the dark springing hair.

The Assembly of the Wondrous Head. But that of course referred to the other Bran, whose head had presided over the feasting of his followers. The Wondrous Head of Bran. A little shiver ran over her and quite suddenly she'd had enough of her own company and that of the well. Picking up brush and pail she ran from the clearing, slopping the black water down the legs of her jeans and liberally dousing the bracken that lined the path. Leaving them outside the back door, she went round the house to make herself presentable before going in to see her mother's friends. She did not notice Mrs Hare through the kitchen window, nor see her pause in the act of filling the teapot, a small satisfied smile hovering round her rather tight mouth.

When Brian arrived at Conningley at six o'clock the other guests had left and Vanessa was in the front garden. She came up to the car as he brought it to a stop outside the door. Since her fantasy earlier in the afternoon she had felt a growing compulsion, ridiculous though she knew it was, to satisfy herself that he was in reality more than just a disembodied head. The wave of relief that swamped her as he climbed out of the car proved the hold that her daydream had taken of her.

"Hello, Uncle Bran!" She reached on tip-toe to kiss his cheek and his arm came swiftly round her shoulders.

"How's my Vanessa?"

"All right." His hand felt hot through the thin cotton of her shirt and she could feel it trembling slightly. "You haven't forgotten about that cream tea, have you?"

"No, but I'm afraid it will have to wait till next week. That's why I haven't been in touch. We've a rush job on and it's impossible for me to leave the office early at the moment."

"Never mind; let's hope it will be worth waiting for!"

"My own sentiments exactly!"

She turned her head at the rather odd note in his voice, but he smiled at her quickly and, reassured, she went happily with him into the house.

The decorators had finished the dining-room and Julia was very pleased with the result. The pale green paper lightened the room beautifully and toned with the emerald velvet curtains and the deep sage of the carpet.

"It'll be like dining in the middle of a forest!" Gavin teased her as they stood surveying the room.

"You do like it, though?"

He bent his head to kiss her. "Of course I do, my darling. Impeccable taste, as always!"

"And you agree we should go ahead and look for some ladder-back chairs?"

"I suppose so, if we can get them at a reasonable price."

"I'll go to *Sandys of Time* tomorrow and see what they advise."

Julia had been to the antique shop several times, and on each occasion it was the pleasant, grey-haired Miss Bingley who had served her. Today however a tall, fair man was standing behind the counter examining a piece of glass through a magnifying glass. This, she assumed, must be Mr Sandys himself. He put the glass down and turned to her with Adam's smile.

"Good afternoon. Are you wanting help or just browsing?"

She smiled back. "Help, please! I'm Julia Prior, from Conningley. I believe I've met your son."

"Oh yes?" Harry Sandys took her hand, searching his memory for any reference the boys might have made but unable to think of one. "He was looking for something for you?" he prompted.

"No, we met socially. That is, he was kind enough to run my daughter home from Wendover Station and stayed for a cup of tea."

"I see." It must have been Adam, then. He hadn't mentioned the incident, Harry was sure, but there was no apparent reason why he should have done. "And what is it you're interested in, Mrs Prior? Glass? Porcelain?"

"No, I'm actually looking for some dining chairs. Ladder-back, if possible."

"Ah, then I might be able to help you. It just happens that I bought half a dozen at an auction last week. Excellent condition, too." He shook his head as Julia's eyes went quickly round the small shop. "They're up at the house. As you can see, we've rather limited space here so we have to keep some of the larger items at home. However, it's only up the road. I could run you there now, if you'd like to see them."

"I'd love to, if it's no trouble."

"None at all. My younger son's working in the room at the back – I'll just let him know where I'm going."

The Sandys' house was at the edge of the village and looked on to fields and spinneys and an uninterrupted view of the Chilterns. Harry opened the front door and stood aside for Julia to enter. The house, she guessed, was not as old as Conningley, late Victorian, probably, with high ceilings and well-proportioned rooms. It had a family atmosphere about it which immediately appealed to her.

"Are you there, Joy? I've brought Mrs Prior to look at some chairs."

Joy Sandys came quickly from the back of the hall. This must be Hilary's mother! She shook her hand, murmuring conventional greetings. Impossible to admit having met her daughter, since she'd promised Adam not to mention her visit in front of his father.

"There are pros and cons to being in the antique business, Mrs Prior," she remarked, leading the way across the hall. "My home is full of beautiful things and I'm free to use any I like, but every now and then one of my favourites is whipped away and sold! Sometimes I'm quite heartbroken!"

The large room at the back of the house had been the original dining-room and made an ideal store, with space to show off the various items of furniture. Julia knew as soon as she saw the chairs that they were exactly what she wanted.

"They are genuine Georgian, aren't they?"

"Yes indeed." Harry Sandys stepped forward. "The colour's always a guide and if you look closely you can see signs of wear along the arm rests and on the stretchers underneath. You don't get that on reproductions."

"They're certainly very handsome. Would it be all right if my husband came to look at them?"

"Of course; any time that's convenient."

"You have some lovely things here, haven't you?" Julia walked slowly round the room, peering into cheval glasses and admiring a magnificent display of crystal.

"You know, of course, that we've several other shops? If

at any time you don't see what you're looking for at Ickfield, it's always worth trying Chesham or Amersham."

"Have you time for a cup of tea, Mrs Prior?" Joy asked suddenly, aware of her husband's faint surprise. "I was just about to make one when you arrived."

"That's very kind. I'd love one."

"I'm afraid you'll have to excuse me," Harry said apologetically. "I left David in charge of the shop and I'm expecting a delivery this afternoon. I want to be there to see it offloaded."

"I met your daughter briefly one evening," Joy remarked, as the two women settled themselves in the sitting-room. "She's a lovely girl: a nurse, isn't she?"

"A doctor, actually. Or at least, almost. She'll be fully qualified when she's done her year as house officer at Rokeby."

"My goodness, I didn't realize that. When Adam mentioned she was working at the hospital, I automatically assumed she'd be nursing. You must be very proud of her."

As though mention of his name had conjured him up, they heard the front door open and a moment later Adam came into the room. His face lit up as he saw Julia.

"Mrs Prior! What a pleasant surprise!"

"I've just fallen for your father's ladder-back chairs!"

"I can't say I blame you – they're magnificent!"

"Sit down, dear, and I'll make some fresh tea," his mother said. "I wasn't expecting you quite so soon."

"I missed the chandeliers." He lowered himself into a chair. "Infuriating, because I know Father wanted them, but the price rocketed way above the limit he'd given me." His eyes went back to Julia. "Any news of Hilary? I've been wondering how she was getting on."

"She phoned last night in a state of complete exhaustion. She's loving the work, though. No doubt we'll hear more when she comes home at the end of next week."

As his mother left the room Adam leaned forward. "Mrs Prior, there's something I wanted to ask you. Did Vanessa mention the diary she found in the summer-house?"

Julia looked at him in surprise. "Diary? Oh yes, I do remember hearing something. Didn't you come round to see her about it?"

"That's right. She asked me to transcribe it because she couldn't read the old-fashioned writing. It's a hundred years old and might be quite valuable. Shall I get it for you?"

He hesitated, wondering whether to elaborate further, but if she read the diary for herself she would make her own assessment of it and the responsibility for deciding whether or not Vanessa should see it would no longer be his.

"I don't know that diaries are much in my line, but I can give it back to Vanessa for you."

Some explanation would be necessary after all. "The fact is," he said slowly, "I've been wondering if it might upset her. It's a bit gruesome in parts – the girl who wrote it was obviously insane."

Julia shuddered. "Then in that case we don't want it back, thank you. If you think it might be valuable, perhaps you could sell it for us."

"Yes, of course. I wonder, though, if I could let a friend of mine see it first? She's the editor of *Chiltern Topics* and would be very interested in doing an article on it. It's local history, after all."

"Certainly, I've no objection."

"And you don't even want to look at it?"

"I don't think so, if it makes unpleasant reading. Just let me know if anyone's interested in buying it."

Adam sat back as his mother returned with the replenished teapot. He found he was quite relieved that Julia hadn't wanted the diary. While he doubted that she was either nervous or over-imaginative, it might well have made her uneasy as it had Hilary, and there was no point in diminishing in any way the pleasure she was taking in her new home. He remembered that she had shown little curiosity in either the Stone or the well in her garden and he was quite happy that this lack of interest should continue. Both her daughters had been affected in varying degrees and that was a sufficient price for one family. And he had cleared the way for Louise, if she wanted to go ahead with the story. He could only hope none of the Priors would read the published article.

Julia, having already dismissed the diary from her mind, had returned to the subject of the chairs. "If Gavin could call round to see them I'd be so grateful," she was saying to Joy Sandys. "He'll phone before he comes, of course, but if I have my way it will be this evening. I'd like to get it settled as soon as possible."

"He can come any time, of course, but don't feel you have to rush. We'd be quite willing to hold them for you while you make up your mind."

Julia rose to her feet. "Thank you, and also for the tea. I must be getting back now, but I hope to be in touch soon. In the meantime, it's very pleasant to have met you."

Adam stood up. "May I run you home?"

"No thanks, it'll only take me a few minutes. And thank you for warning me about the diary, Adam. It certainly doesn't sound the kind of thing I'd be happy for Vanessa to read. She's at rather an impressionable age at the moment."

He watched her through the windows as she walked with his mother to the gate. So Hilary would be at home at the end of next week. Despite his resolutions to put her out of his mind, he knew that he would do everything in his power to see her again.

Louise sighed as she laid down her library book and went through to put the kettle on. One of the penalties of having a flat in the centre of Aylesbury was that one's relations, exhausted after a Saturday afternoon's shopping, were liable to drop in without warning for refreshment. Tracy followed her into the kitchenette.

"If you ever have a daughter, never be persuaded to go

shopping with her for shoes!"

"As you well know, sister dear, I have no intention of having a daughter."

"You'll change your mind, when the right man comes along!" Tracy said, with the infuriating complacency of the married. Louise did not reply. The right man had come – and gone – but here she still was. The passing thought took her by surprise. Did it imply that if Adam had asked her to marry him, she might have accepted? Perhaps – perhaps not. The arrangement they had had suited her to perfection – as it had him, until recently – and she would have been only too happy for it to continue.

"What have you been doing since I last saw you?" she asked, to change the subject. "Apart, that is, from trudging round shoe shops?"

"Not much really. Linda, Rona, Moira and I went to Ickfield on Tuesday, to salve our joint conscience over Marion."

"At Ickfield?"

"Julia had her round. She's made us all feel pretty uncomfortable, I can tell you. We really should have done something about seeing her all this time. Quite apart from the sheer obligation of it, she's still jolly good company, as astringent as ever."

"And was the beautiful Hilary present?" Louise asked steadily, pouring the boiling water into the pot.

"No, she's working at the hospital now. Incidentally, she's broken off her engagement to that doctor. Julia seems to think it was a mistake from the word 'go'."

For a long moment Louise stood motionless, the kettle still in her hand. Then with an effort she put it down, dropped the lid on to the teapot and turned to her sister.

"Right," she said brightly, "shall we go through?"

Fourteen

There was talk in the village of blood being found on the Druid Stone and among the older inhabitants, better versed in local legend, a certain amount of knowing nods of the head. Trouble was brewing up again, see if it wasn't, and they'd all sleep easier in their beds once the Stone was appeased. But who would the victim be this time? They avoided each other's eyes and went out of their way to disguise the fact that they no longer took their dogs for walks along the hill-top.

In the shops and cottages and along the cobbled old streets, an increasing sense of disquiet prevailed, a feeling of marking time till disaster struck. November it was, last time, November 1880, but the consensus of opinion was that they wouldn't have to wait till autumn on this occasion. Things were stepping up and were bound to culminate soon. In the meantime the wisest course was to keep your head down, go quietly about your business and remember to say your prayers at night. It did no harm to take precautions and the vicar, a relatively new incumbent, was surprised and gratified at the steady increase in his congregation. He didn't appear to notice that some of his older parishioners bobbed a little curtsey towards the Green Man carved on the end of the pews as well as to the altar. Old beliefs died hard hereabouts, especially when the Stone was stirring, and it was as well to hedge your bets.

No hint of any of this unease reached the family at Conningley, but Vanessa in her intermittent periods of clarity was also aware that the climax was fast approaching and a sick excitement possessed her which, when it passed, she was at a loss to understand. Meanwhile Mrs Hare, lips tightly compressed, continued while she could to hold the Power at bay with offerings of chickens and rabbits.

On the Wednesday of the next week Brian at last phoned Vanessa.

"I'm finally redeeming my promise of a cream tea," he told her. "How would Friday suit you?"

"Fine, thanks."

"Can you come into the office to meet me? It would save having to trail out to Ickfield first."

"Yes of course. What time?"

"Considering the long hours I've put in for the last ten days, I should feel quite justified in leaving at four. And Vanessa –" his hand tightened on the receiver. "Would you do something for me? Would you wear that pretty stone pendant? It's so unusual I'd like to examine it more closely."

In the hall at Conningley Vanessa's eyes glazed over suddenly. She couldn't – she couldn't really. It wasn't hers to wear when and if she chose. It was sacred, lent to her in trust for a specific purpose –

"Van?" His voice was strident in her ear. "Will you, please?"

"I'm – not sure where it is," she lied wildly, feeling it jostle against her thigh in the pocket of her jeans.

"Please," he said again hoarsely. "It's – important."

"I'll see." Her voice was scarcely above a whisper, and with that he had to be content. He put down the phone, the sweat coursing down his face as he flayed himself mercilessly for so blatantly inviting temptation. For he knew instinctively that when she wore that stone she became the Other, the one he worshipped and desired so feverishly. And how could what he did to that Other harm Vanessa herself? She would know nothing as long as the stone stayed round her neck. He acknowledged that the whole concept was evil, illogical, that madness lay only a hair's breadth away, but he could no longer deny himself one last chance of possessing her.

Last chance? He paused in the act of wiping his streaming face. Why should he suppose this chance to be his last? Because of the possibility that he had not after all convinced Gavin and Julia of his sanity? If they should suspect, even remotely, how his mind was working, he would never be allowed near Vanessa again.

Friday. Two more days. Somehow he would have to live through them.

As soon as he saw her, standing shyly by the desk in the outer office, he realized she was not wearing the stone. For a moment blind fury shook him, misting his eyes. Then, forcing himself to be calm, he reasoned that of course she had it with her. The Other one could hardly be expected to walk into his office and speak politely to Miss Blake. Hysterical laughter welled in his throat, and that too he fought down.

"Hello Vane sa!" he exclaimed heartily. "I hope you've worked up a good appetite!" And with his hand on her shoulder he steered her quickly out of the office and down the stairs. Come to think of it, there was nothing to be gained in her wearing the stone yet. It was to Vanessa he had promised the tea, and she must be allowed to enjoy it. That was only fair. It was afterwards, when, perhaps, they went for a walk down the country lanes – then would be the time to slip the pendant round her neck and plead, cajole, beg –

He gritted his teeth and, opening the car door, let her climb inside. She glanced back over her shoulder a little apprehensively. Obviously, despite himself he was behaving strangely. Control, control! He switched on the ignition, reversed quickly, and almost hit the car parked behind. Swearing under his breath he manoeuvred his way out of the car-park and through the busy afternoon streets to the relatively clear Tring Road. Vanessa sat quietly beside him and he glanced surreptitiously at her pointed little face and untidy hair. This was Vanessa, who all her life had seemed like a daughter to him. It was about this child that he was having such dark imaginings. Oh God, help him! The car swerved, straightened, and rushed on and after a moment, to obviate the need to make conversation, he switched on the radio. Swelling and magnificent, the majestic notes of the 'New World' Symphony poured into the car: and Vanessa said in a small voice, "Could we have it on Radio One, do you think?"

"Yes, yes of course, if you can find it."

She leant forward, her hair screening her face, and out of the corner of his eye he watched her fingers with their raggedly bitten nails move the knob to the position she wanted. Banal chit-chat, pop songs. With a small, contented sigh she leaned back and he realized that the very triteness of the programme, known and familiar, had in some way soothed her apprehension. He drew a deep breath. As she was now, she was safe enough, God knew. She had nothing to fear from him. He *loved* her, damn it, loved her with an altogether sane and normal love of many years' standing. He was her Uncle Bran. His hands quivered on the wheel, for that, oddly enough, was the name the Other also used.

On the far side of Tring he took the fork off the main road and soon they were away from all signs of habitation in the superbly rolling countryside of the foothills. Vanessa, more relaxed now, was softly singing in accompaniment with the radio. They had reached the village and he circled the green, with its pond and sixteenth-century stocks and drew up in the square. As he switched off the engine, and with it the radio, silence engulfed them, the peaceful calm of the country broken only by the soft clucking of hens in the farmyard opposite.

"O.K.?"

She nodded and climbed out of the car. A young fifteen, Marion had said, and he achingly agreed. Tall and straight, thin rather than slim, faded T-shirt and tattered jeans. He was sure Julia had not caught sight of her before she left home!

They went together into the little tea-shop, Brian bending his head to avoid the low beams. There were people at several of the tables. Vanessa went across to an empty one and he sat down opposite her. No sign of the Other – but that was as it should be. Soon, soon, in the winding country lanes beyond the village, he would slip the stone round her neck and gaze again into those fathomless, all-knowing eyes.

The order was given; the tea arrived: freshly baked scones still warm from the oven, home-made strawberry jam and mounds of rich cream. Somehow he managed to eat one scone and passed the other to Vanessa.

"How clever of you to know of this place, Uncle Bran! Have you been here before?" She ladled still more cream on to the already top-heavy scone and angled it expertly into her mouth.

"No, I – I heard about it from someone in the office."

"It's lovely, isn't it? I must tell Nick to bring Amanda."

"Amanda?" Brian echoed blankly. His eyes were on her face, watching in case there should be a glimpse, a sign that the Other one was there, waiting for him.

"Amanda Pembrook. He's taking her to the gliding club dance tonight. I wonder if he's all soppy with her! I can't imagine Nick with girls!"

Brian licked his lips. "Haven't you any boy friends, Van?"

She shook her head. "Boys that age are so silly!"

"And – older ones?"

"They don't notice me," she said frankly. "I used to go to discos and things in Newcastle with Pam, my friend, but we always freaked out together."

"I see," said Brian, who didn't. The two cups of tea he had drunk to pass the time had made him hot. Coming straight from the office as he had, he was wearing a dark suit and tie and all at once felt uncomfortably formal. He should have left his jacket in the car, rolled up his shirt sleeves.

Vanessa had finished at last and sat back with a sigh of deep contentment. "It was very kind of you to bring me here. I really enjoyed it."

"Good. I'm sorry there was such a time-lapse after the invitation."

They walked slowly across the hot square towards the car. Brian's heart was hammering, his mouth dry.

"Shall we stroll round and look at the village? There's no hurry, is there? I'll just leave my jacket in the car."

She made no demur, waiting while he tossed it in and then walking happily enough beside him as they looked at the stocks, the old cottages, with their colourful front gardens. Casually, so casually, he was edging her towards a little-used lane which, twisting and turning, gave access through barred gates to long-grassed meadows screened by high hedges and drystone walls. This he knew, because he had taken the trouble to drive out here the previous evening to scout out the land.

The afternoon sun beat down from a cloudless sky, scorching his shoulders through the thin shirt. And it was then, so near to his goal, that the first serious doubt came to him and he said harshly, breaking into her conversation, "You have got it with you, haven't you, Van? The pendant?"

And at once, from the way her eyes fell, he knew that she had not. He could feel the breath rasping his throat like emery paper.

"Why?" he whispered. "Why, when I asked you so particularly?"

Her eyes were wide and frightened. "I'm sorry, Uncle Bran, but I don't really like wearing it very much. It makes me feel funny, somehow. And it's not mine, you see. I was afraid of losing it."

The full extent of his betrayal burst over him and he seized her shoulders, shaking her violently. "But I need it –

I need *her*! Don't you understand? You should! It was you she used to trap me in the first place! Don't you remember, that night at Conningley?"

She said on a high note, "Please don't, Uncle Bran! You're hurting me!"

He didn't hear her. He was gripping her shoulders, staring into her eyes with a crazed expression that terrified her.

"You're there, aren't you? Why don't you show yourself? I won't hurt the child! The stone isn't necessary – come to me – now – please! Please don't make me suffer like this!"

He pulled her violently towards him, his mouth closing on her neck, and she screamed, high and shrill, sending him reeling back as sanity blunderingly returned. And as his grip loosened she turned and started to run wildly, weaving from side to side, back towards the village. He caught her in two strides, horror, remorse and fear struggling for supremacy. What had he done? God, where was that celebrated control now?

"Van – no, sweetie, don't look like that, I'm not going to hurt you! Van, please forgive me! I'm sorry – I wouldn't have – I don't know what –"

Disjointed and distraught, the half sentences spilled from him while he held her against her struggling, trying to calm her as though she were a panic-stricken animal.

"Van, I wouldn't have frightened you for the world, you know that. It wasn't *you* I was speaking to!"

She said through shaking lips, "But there was no-one else there."

"No." No-one else there. That was the trouble, the cause of his disintegration. He looked at her imploringly and saw that it was no use. By that momentary madness back in the lane he had destroyed everything that had been between them over the last ten years or more. Vanessa, his little dream-daughter, was staring at him as though he were a stranger.

He said thickly, "I'll take you home."

Side by side, each of them staring straight ahead, they drove back in total silence, without even the radio to provide a semblance of normality. He knew she was tense, braced to defend herself against him if necessary, but as they turned into Ickfield High Street and she realized the ordeal was almost over, she said very quietly, "I'm so sorry, Uncle Bran."

"*You're* sorry!" The words jolted out of him, more bitter than he'd intended. "For what, may I ask?"

"About – about Auntie Marion. It must be – very hard for you."

He didn't trust himself to reply and he knew, loathing himself almost beyond bearing, that her tears were very near. Deciding against the drive and the risk of an invitation from Julia, he stopped at the gate and waited, not looking at her, for her to go. She leaned across suddenly and kissed his cheek.

"Thank you for the cream tea!" she said in a rush, and ran quickly up the drive.

He knew what she meant, of course: that she'd forgiven him the unforgivable. Sweet, generous, uncomprehending Vanessa. The tears were streaming down his own face. He couldn't go home in this state. Driving slowly because he could scarcely see, he went round the crescent back on to the main road and almost immediately turned off in the direction of the gliding club. If he parked his car among all the others it would not give rise to comment and he could walk on the hill until he was able to face himself and the outside world again. Impatiently brushing the tears from his face, he turned up the long dusty driveway leading to the club.

"Van? Is that you, darling? Did you have a nice –"

Julia broke off as Vanessa went flying past her up the stairs, her face ravaged with tears.

"Vanessa! What is it?" Julia set off at a run after her, catching the bedroom door as it swung violently to and

Vanessa flung herself face down across the bed.

"Darling, what happened?" Julia leaned distractedly over her, stroking the long, tangled hair and heaving shoulders. "What's the matter? Please tell me!"

But Vanessa was too incoherent to explain and it was some time before even a hint of the trouble reached Julia.

"Uncle Bran's *ill*!" she sobbed at last. "He's much, much worse than we thought!"

"He didn't hurt you?" Julia broke in sharply, all her latent fears instantly resurrected.

"No, no he—"

"Vanessa answer me! He didn't make any attempt to —"

She looked up then and met her mother's anxious eyes. "No, he didn't. But I think he wanted to."

"Oh my God!" said Julia softly. "And to think I let you go with him!" She pulled the girl against her, cradling her with fierce protectiveness. "Darling, you are telling me the truth? Nothing happened?"

"Nothing. Really." Shudderingly Vanessa blocked the thought of his hot, feverish lips on her neck. "He – didn't know what he was doing, though, Mummy. That's what frightened me. When I – when he *did* realize, he was horrified."

Julia longed to know exactly what had happened, but the child was too distraught to be pestered for details at this stage. Suffice to know that no harm had come to her. Oh Brian, how *could* you? *Vanessa*! She would never be able to forgive him for that.

Nick said anxiously, "You are enjoying it, Amanda?"

She laughed, tossing back her hair. "It's not exactly what you'd call groovy, is it?"

"I'm sorry. I didn't think it would be *quite* so old-hat."

"Oh, it's all right for a giggle. Claire and Steve seem to be enjoying themselves, anyway." She nodded as the couple circled slowly past, their arms wound round each other.

Nick grunted agreement. Steve hadn't required much

pushing to date Claire after all, and she seemed to be considerably more amenable to his overtures than Amanda was to his own.

"What time did you say your father's collecting you?"

"Eleven-thirty."

"Pity really. It's after ten now."

"I think it's jolly decent of him. You couldn't have got us home, could you?"

"Oh, I know. I didn't mean that. It's just –" he broke off. "I mean –"

"I know exactly what you mean, Nick Prior!"

She was playing with him, he thought resentfully. She probably didn't really like him at all. She didn't even let him kiss her properly, and he'd botched the last attempt. Truth to tell, he was aware that she'd had more experience than he had, and was afraid of looking a fool. But she really was very pretty, and all the other boys looked at her wherever they went. It was worth a lot just to be with her.

'Your famous club's rather tatty, isn't it?"

"I suppose it is, yes. I've only been in the club house once before. Most of the time we're out with the gliders, steadying the wings before take-off and so on."

"Big deal!"

Nick flushed. "Look, if you're so all-fired bored –"

She bent forward quickly, taking hold of his hand, and the remembered hotness, still new and unusual enough to take him by surprise, washed over him.

"There, there, I was only teasing! You play with your aeroplanes all you want to!"

He said with an effort, "Shall we go outside for a bit?"

"Why?" The direct challenge again.

This time he met her eyes squarely. "So we can neck, of course!"

She burst out laughing. "What an irresistible prospect!"

"Well, shall we?"

"I'll come for a *walk*."

"O.K. Suit yourself."

It was cool after the heat of the buildings and the sky was an archway of scudding clouds. Side by side, not touching each other, they started to stroll along the deserted field. On their right the long low shapes of the hangars were huddled together and on the far skyline the Druid Stone stood up like a finger.

"You know about the Stone?" he asked, breaking the silence. It occurred to him that she was waiting now for him to make a pass at her. Well, she could damn well wait.

"What stone?" She shivered slightly but he didn't take the hint.

"The one over there. It's supposed to come down and drink at our well on Midsummer Day."

"You're making it up!"

"No I'm not. It's an ancient monument and there are all kinds of weird stories about it. You should ask our daily! And there was a kid in the post office a few weeks ago who insisted it up and hit him!"

"The *stone* did?"

"Yes. And he'd a large bruise to show for it, too."

"How spooky! Can we go and have a look at it?"

"It's farther away than you think – right at the end of the flight path. You're not wearing the right shoes for walking."

"Then I'll take them off," said Amanda, suiting the action to the words. "Tell me more – I'm in the mood for ghost stories!"

"Apparently people used to be sacrificed on it in the old days, according to Adam Sandys."

"And who's Adam Sandys?" Amanda fell into step beside him again, swinging her sandals by their straps.

"A friend of my sister's. He'd make your hair curl with all his talk of severed heads and things. Apparently the head was a very widespread cult among the Celts. A skull was found in our well."

"Recently, you mean?"

"Fairly. I'm not sure exactly when it was excavated."

Her bare arm brushed against him, more, he thought, by design than accident, but again he ignored it. On their left a glider lay secured and Amanda glanced at it as they passed.

"How do those things get off the ground? They haven't any engines, have they?"

"No, they're pulled by the winch cable until they gain a height of about six hundred feet or so, then they drop the cable. And sometimes they're catapulted up."

"How long do they stay in the air?"

"It depends on the wind currents. Two or three minutes, usually."

She stopped and stared at him. "Two or three *minutes*? All that fuss for two or three *minutes*?"

"Well, of course the larger clubs have powered aircraft to tow them. Then you can go much higher and stay up for twenty minutes or more."

"Good grief! I thought you were up for the whole afternoon!"

"That would be far too expensive. Each ascent costs a bomb as it is."

She was silent for a moment. "And those winch things rush along the field pulling the gliders behind them?"

"Oh no, they're stationary. There's one often up by the Stone, though they don't use it every day. The cable is run back to the glider by a truck and fastened on to it. Then, when the glider's ready for take-off, someone signals the winch driver, who takes up the slack. The signalling's done by orange bats, because as you can see it's quite a long way away. You need that length of cable to get the thing off the ground."

"Oh."

Perhaps he'd been too technical. She seemed to have lost interest and a moment later she said sullenly, "I didn't know we came out here for a lecture on gliding!"

The unfairness of it stung him. "But you asked me!"

"Well, I think we should be turning back now."

"I thought you wanted to see the Stone."

"I've changed my mind. I can see it well enough from here, and I'm getting cold. Damn!"

"What is it?"

She was standing on one foot, rubbing her bare toes. "I scratched my foot on a bramble."

"Poor Amanda! But you did say you wanted a walk."

"And you wanted something else, I seem to remember!"

Elation filled him. He'd won a round at last! He reached for her and she came quickly into his arms, and this time it was perfect, wonderful, magic – her mouth soft and warm, her arms tightly round his neck and the wind blowing her sweet-smelling hair across his face. After a while she turned her head away and he felt her stiffen, her fingers digging into his shoulders.

"Nick! There's someone watching us! Oh, how horrible!"

He turned quickly, staring as she had in the direction of the Stone, and between themselves and the monument was the unmistakable figure of a man, seemingly gazing in their direction. He felt the gooseflesh prickle his skin.

"Come on!" He seized Amanda's hand and started to half run with her back towards the safety of the club.

"Oh Nick, wait! I'm not wearing shoes, remember – slow down!"

He glanced back over his shoulder but the figure hadn't moved. "O.K. Put your sandals on."

Leaning against him she did so, struggling in the uncertain light with the straps and buckles. "Whoever was it? What was he doing up there?"

"I don't know." But it was the second half of her question he was answering, because he was almost sure who the figure had been. After all, he'd seen him up here before.

"What was that?" Julia started up on one elbow.

"Relax, darling. It's only Nick coming home from the

dance. Go back to sleep."

"I haven't been to sleep." Julia lay down again, pulling the sheet over her shoulder.

"Still worrying about Brian?"

"What do you think?"

"You know, you may have got it all out of proportion. It's not at all clear what exactly happened this afternoon."

"It was enough to upset Vanessa considerably."

"Yes, but she's very fond of Brian. Anything that seemed to point to the fact that he was ill would upset her. She may not have realized just what you were asking."

"Nonsense. Van may be young for her age, but she's not an imbecile. She knew, all right. Can you imagine how she must have felt – a man she's known most of her life, old enough to be her father?"

"I still can't believe he'd do anything to hurt her. It just doesn't make sense."

"And that is precisely my point. It *doesn't* make sense. She said herself that he didn't seem to know what he was doing, and when he *did* realize he was terribly upset."

"There you are, then."

"That's supposed to make me feel better? Gavin, the man's going out of his mind! One thing's sure anyway. He's not coming to this house again."

"But we're his friends – we can't just abandon him! He can't help it if he's ill."

"I hope very much for his sake that he gets better soon, but in the meantime I repeat he's not coming here. Mind you, I doubt if he'd dare to anyway, after this afternoon."

"And what will you tell Marion?"

"It's up to Brian to explain if anyone has to. Thank goodness I had her over during the week. Having started that, I can go on with it and avoid having Brian."

"He'd have to come and collect her."

"That would only take minutes and you'd be here. Even so, any time he's in the house, Vanessa stays in her room. I'm not going to have her upset like that again. In the meantime, for pity's sake get him to a doctor. He's agreed in principle, and now it really is a matter of urgency."

Gavin put his arm round her. "Calm down now, sweetheart, or you're never going to get any sleep."

"But you will do something?"

"Yes, I'll do something, but don't rush me. I'll have to play it very carefully. If he won't go voluntarily we can't force him. Now stop worrying. Van's all right. She's come to no harm, thank God, and now that we suspect what's happening we can take appropriate steps to safeguard her. Poor devil, though, can you imagine how he must be feeling?"

"No," said Julia. "I'm glad to say that I can't."

Fifteen

The days crawled past. Vanessa's experience had not been mentioned again and Brian had so far managed to evade Gavin's suggestions of meeting for lunch. If to her mother's eyes Vanessa herself seemed pale and withdrawn, at least there had been no further tears. Rona Laidlaw phoned with a return invitation to tea.

"We've decided to make it a regular arrangement, each of us taking turns. Marion's agreed to come."

But Julia excused herself on the grounds of a previous engagement. She didn't want to see Marion just at the moment.

'I'm going into Aylesbury, Van," she called up the stairs. "Like to come with me?"

"Not today, thanks."

"You all right, darling?"

"Fine."

Julia shrugged and picked up the car keys. From her bedroom window Vanessa watched her drive through the gateway and her hand went to her pocket for the spell-stones. The prickling sensation when she touched them had died away now that they were so used to each other. She stroked the tolmaen thoughtfully, her nail tracing the stylized line drawing of the hare. Why had Uncle Bran wanted her to wear it so much? For that matter, how had he even known she had it? And what would have happened if she had ignored all her instincts and taken it along as he'd requested?

She was aware of a gentle humming sound, and dreamily slipped the thong over her head. At the same moment the bedroom door opened and Mrs Hare stood there.

She said softly: "You know what must be done?"

Vanessa nodded, her glazed eyes fixed on the other woman.

"The Stone grows impatient."

"I know."

"It must be this week. You realize the importance of that?"

"I do."

"Only once was the sacrifice delayed too long, and on that occasion half the village was destroyed, with heavy loss of life."

"I remember."

Mrs Hare stared at her a moment longer. Then, satisfied, nodded and quietly left the room. Her own preparations were also complete. All personal belongings from the last two years – and they had been very few – had now been disposed of. In the garden shed a couple of wood pigeons, their soft purple feathers limp, waited to play their part in eking out the minor sacrifices till the end of the week. Everything was ready and it would be a relief, after all the mounting tension, when the deed was accomplished once more.

With her mind lapping excitedly round the imminent

prospect of blood, Mrs Hare returned to washing the breakfast dishes.

Hilary arrived home in time for breakfast on the Saturday morning. Her Italian tan had faded considerably and there were purple shadows under her eyes.

"You look in need of a hospital bed yourself!" her father greeted her.

"A bed, certainly! I intend to have a lovely, relaxing weekend. I do like the decorations, by the way. Doesn't the new paper make a difference?"

"I hope you also appreciate the chair you're sitting on. Your mother went mad! Just as well my premium bonds came up last month!"

"Don't listen to him!" Julia retorted. "He fell for them as much as I did."

"They're certainly very elegant. Where did you find them?"

Julia glanced at her, but she was intent on her grapefruit. "Through Mr Sandys. Adam was asking after you."

"Oh?"

"He also mentioned the diary Vanessa'd lent him and asked if I wanted it back. From his description it sounded rather unpleasant, so I said no."

Hilary's hand tightened fractionally on her spoon. "Yes, it was. I read it myself."

The door rocked open as Nick came into the room. "Hi, Doc! What's noo?"

"Do you really want to hear?"

"The gory details? No thanks, you keep 'em. Mum, could I have a packed lunch today? Amanda and I are going to Woburn."

"It's rather short notice but I suppose we can rustle up something."

"We only decided last night." Nick poured a mountain of cornflakes into his plate. "What are you doing today, Hilary? Going back to bed?"

"You too! I must obviously look worse than I feel! No, Nick, I'm not going to bed, but I'm certainly not going to overtax myself. A leisurely stroll to the village to buy some tights, and then I think a deck-chair in the garden will suit me nicely."

It was very pleasant, she reflected half an hour later, to stroll along in the sunshine without having to keep glancing at her watch or worry about what she was supposed to be doing. Even so she hadn't completely disengaged herself from her other existence and her mind was still circling round the patient she'd seen barely two hours earlier; which was why she didn't notice Adam's car draw up alongside until he called her name.

"Sorry, Adam, I was miles away! How are you?"

"In need of medical attention! Have you anything planned for today?"

"Not really."

"Come with me, then. I'm on my way to an auction the other side of Oxford. It should be an interesting sale and it's a perfect day for a drive."

"That sounds very tempting. Thanks, I'd like to."

"Good. We can stop somewhere for a meal on the way back, and make a day of it."

"I'll have to go home first, and let them know."

"Of course."

As he leaned over to open the door for her he noticed she wasn't wearing her ring. Perhaps they didn't encourage jewellery at the hospital but he'd have expected her to put it on as soon as she arrived home. At Conningley he waited while she hurried inside with her purchases, whistling contentedly under his breath. She was looking tired. No doubt they were overworking her. She came hurrying out of the door and slipped into the seat beside him.

"All fixed. Where exactly is it we're going?"

"To a private house just outside Woodstock. I went over yesterday for the preview. It belongs to the Darcey family but death duties are forcing them to sell almost everything.

It's a sad business but of course I have to gather with the rest of the vultures."

"Are you after anything in particular?"

"Father's very keen to acquire some chandeliers. We missed them at an auction I went to last week. Personally I loathe the things. Can't imagine why anyone buys them."

"I believe you were responsible for providing our new dining chairs?"

"Indirectly. Do you like them?"

"Very much." She paused. "Mother mentioned that you'd asked her about the diary."

"Yes. I don't mind admitting I was relieved when she told me to keep it."

"Have you shown it to Louise?"

"Not yet, but she wants to borrow the transcript. She's thinking of doing a follow-up feature on it. You wouldn't have any objection would you?"

"Not unless people started arriving in hordes demanding a guided tour of Conningley!"

He laughed. "Admittedly that would be rather disconcerting. Incidentally, when I saw Vanessa in the village she didn't mention the diary at all."

"Perhaps she doesn't want it back either."

"That would solve a lot of problems." But she had kept the spell-stones. 'Until I get my O-level results' she'd said. That would probably be in another week or two now and then he would have to ask her for them, even at the risk of reminding her about the diary. They were of considerable historical interest and their return would cause a big stir in the village – and no doubt round off Louise's story very satisfactorily.

Hilary leaned her head back against the soft leather and watched the scenery rushing past. They were on the motorway now and the noise of their progress made conversation more difficult. She thought contentedly that there was nowhere in the world she would rather be than here beside Adam driving through this lovely countryside.

Was it by accident that they had met in the High Street, or had he engineered it? And had he thought as much as she had in the intervening weeks of that swift, hard kiss at Conningley gate? There was still Louise, she reminded herself, and he'd apparently seen her recently.

"The lots I'm interested in won't be coming up till this afternoon," Adam remarked as they turned into the ring road round Oxford, "but we can have another look round first if you'd like to. It's a fascinating old house."

"As Vanessa would say, what do we do about lunch?"

"There are several good pubs round about, but there'll be outside caterers in the house or grounds, selling coffee and sandwiches. That might be the best bet; we can relax in the gardens until it's time to go inside."

Darcey Hall was an imposing Queen Anne house set in six acres of land. An attendant was stationed at the gates to direct the steady stream of cars and vans which were beginning to form a queue outside. Having parked in the allotted space, they walked up the remainder of the impeccably gravelled drive to the house itself. Adam showed his catalogue which admitted two and they followed the crowd through the open doorway into the hall. The sound of the auctioneer's voice reached them from the long drawing-room but Adam took her elbow and steered her towards the magnificent staircase, and for the next hour or so they wandered from room to room consulting the catalogue while Adam checked the notes he'd made the previous day. From time to time they met someone he knew, and a discussion would follow on whether some piece had had restoration work done on it, or how much certain lots had gone for that morning.

To Hilary, however, there was an incipient air of sadness about the proceedings. All these treasures had been lovingly gathered together by different members of the family over who knew how many generations, and now, owing to the pressures of modern-day taxation, they were being scattered again. She stood staring into one of the show-cases where a few personal trinkets had been assembled together with more valuable pieces of silver. Among them was a pretty little coral ring in an antique setting surrounded by seed pearls, and she felt her eyes smart as she looked at it.

Adam came up behind her. "Ready to move on?"

"I suppose so. I think I must be more tired than I realized. I'm becoming quite maudlin!"

"Why?"

"It seems so pathetic, having to part with all this." She gestured towards the trinkets. "Just think of the sentiment that must be attached to these – that perfect little ring, for example. Who bought it, and for whom? It probably meant a great deal to both of them, and now it has to go under the hammer with everything else. I can see why you feel like a vulture. I don't think I like auctions very much."

He took her arm. "It is a bit depressing, I know. You just have to be businesslike about it and close your mind to the personal aspect – like being a doctor, I imagine! Come on, let's go and find some lunch."

The sunshine outside seemed extra bright after the cool, dim rooms. Having collected their coffee and sandwiches they moved off across the grass which was now dotted with groups of people similarly engaged. Adam stopped in front of a large octagonal rose bed.

"This all right?"

"Fine." She sat down on the grass and he handed her a cup of coffee.

"Where's that beautiful sapphire ring?" he asked before he could stop himself.

Her eyes dropped. "In a drawer waiting to be handed back to Chris."

He stared down incredulously at her bent head and she added in a low voice, "We came to a mutual agreement to call it off."

The silence seemed to stretch between them. Adam sat down next to her and handed her the packet of sandwiches.

"I suppose I should say I'm sorry," he said at last, "but it wouldn't be true. Unless, of course, you're unhappy about it."

"No." She drew a deep breath. "Well, have you decided how many lots you're going to bid for? Those frightful chandeliers, of course. What else?"

He forced himself to make some sort of reply but his mind was spinning. The world had suddenly flung back its boundaries and nothing was impossible.

When they had finished eating Hilary lay back on the grass and closed her eyes. Within two minutes he saw she was asleep and his eyes softened. She'd probably intended to spend a restful day relaxing in the garden, instead of which he'd rushed her off on an exhausting and rather emotional tour of a big house. Still, there was half an hour before they need go back inside and he asked nothing better than to spend it quietly watching her as she slept.

It was very hot and high above them the speck of an aeroplane crawled across the sky like some celestial honey-bee, its sleepy drone reaching them only intermittently. Adam was filled with a deep sense of happiness, almost frightening in its intensity.

He was still watching her when her eyes opened suddenly, catching the unguarded expression on his face. For a long minute they looked at each other. Neither of them spoke, but both were aware that in that moment they had drawn imperceptibly closer together. She stirred and sat up.

"I'm terribly sorry – what an awful thing to do! My eyes just wouldn't stay open a moment longer."

"It will have done you good. We'd better be making our way back now, though."

After the first hour or so of trying unsuccessfully to discover who was doing the bidding, Hilary lost interest. The prices went rocketing astronomically high and she was glad that the Darceys' sacrifices would at least bring them a good return. She gathered from Adam's occasional movements beside her that he was joining in the bidding, but whether or not he was successful she had no idea.

Her thoughts drifted. She'd wondered whether he would remark on the fact that she wasn't wearing a ring. Chris – What a relief that he'd agreed so readily with her decision. Perhaps he had found someone else too.

Too? Her drooping eyes flicked open for a moment before she allowed them to close again. What was the sense in pretending? She knew she was on the verge of loving Adam, and despite the enigmatic Louise she was almost sure he felt the same. Though she had not wanted to admit it, the attraction had been between them from their first meeting, strengthening considerably on each of the few occasions they had met. Impossible to accept that this was only the fourth time they'd been together.

"Hilary?" Her eyes jerked open to see him smiling at her. "You can wake up now, it's over!"

"Did you get what you wanted?"

"Most of it. Shall we walk round the grounds while they sort things out here?"

The sun was lower in the sky, almost at eye level. It seemed entirely natural for Adam to take her hand. They walked slowly, talking only sporadically, looking at the exquisitely arranged flower-beds, the statues on the terraces, the little lake with the graceful long-necked swans. Eventually they came round in a wide arc to the house again and Adam went inside to collect such purchases as he was taking back with him. By the time they reached the car most of the others had gone.

As Adam switched on the ignition he tossed a small box into her lap.

"What's this?"

"A little reward for staying awake most of the time!"

She knew before she opened it what it must be, but as she lifted the lid to see the coral ring nestling against its cream velvet her eyes filled with tears. "Oh, Adam!"

"You seemed to fall for it, and I'm sure the previous

owner couldn't ask for a better successor."

"Thank you. Thank you." She leaned across to kiss his cheek, slipped the ring on to her right hand and held it up for him to see. "It fits perfectly."

"I hope you're not too tired for a meal out? We could go straight home if you'd rather."

"No; as you tactfully pointed out, I've caught up with some sleep this afternoon!"

"If you're sure then, I know a rather good restaurant where we can have a leisurely meal. They specialize in fish but there's a wide selection of other things too."

An hour or so later they were seated in an attractive little bar with long cold drinks in front of them.

"May I ask a rather personal question?" Adam said suddenly, swirling the ice round in his glass.

"Of course."

"Did you break off your engagement because you realized you'd made a mistake, or because you found you're not ready to tie yourself down at the moment?"

"Because we don't love each other any more."

"And no other corollaries?"

"None."

He drew a deep breath. "Thank you. Now, tell me about the hospital. What exactly is it you're doing at the moment?"

"General medicine. I decided to do what we call 'split posts', which means subdividing medicine and surgery into General Medicine and Paediatrics, followed by General Surgery and Gynaecology."

"And what are you hoping to do at the end of the year?"

"Originally I'd intended to specialize in tropical diseases, but I've always been more interested in Gynae. If I decide to go ahead with that I'll try for a post as Senior House Officer."

"At Rokeby?"

"If they'd have me, certainly."

"That's a relief! I had visions of having to track you

down all over the country!"

A waiter approached with menu cards and when they later resumed their conversation it was, as though by tacit agreement, on less personal subjects. Possibly due to her tiredness, the evening seemed to Hilary to have no beginning and no end. It was as though they'd always been sitting opposite each other at the small corner table with the lamplight leaving their faces in shadow but glowing softly on her coral ring. Around them people came and went and still they sat, leaning towards each other, talking, remaining silent, and spinning out the meal with countless cups of coffee. But at last it was time to go and the spell was broken.

Out in the car-park it was cool and a new moon hung slender and uncertain in the sky. Adam switched on the car radio and they drove without speaking, listening to the dreamy haunting songs and wrapped in their own thoughts. Only when they had passed through Thame did he break the silence.

"What time tomorrow do you have to be back?"

"Not till the evening. About eight o'clock."

"May I see you then?"

"Of course."

"For how long?"

"Come and spend the day at Conningley, if you'd like to. The family won't mind, but I really ought to be with them too. I've hardly seen them today."

"Considering how little time we've spent together," he said quietly, "I've missed you more than I'd have believed possible. This time is going to be worse than ever. I'm beginning to get withdrawal symptoms already."

"We still have tomorrow," she said softly.

"Can you only get home on alternate weekends?"

"I suppose I could manage an occasional evening but I'm 'on take' one out of two, and pretty exhausted the rest of the time."

"I could at least phone you?"

"Yes, I can let you know the best times."

After a moment he said abruptly. "You know, I hadn't meant to say any of that. Having only just extricated yourself from one entanglement, I imagine the last thing you want is to be hounded again so soon."

"I wouldn't say that," she murmured.

He reached for her hand. "The truth of the matter is that since I first caught sight of you, somewhere between Amersham and Great Missenden, I haven't been able to think of anyone or anything else. I suspect I'm not telling you anything you don't know. It must have been pretty obvious."

She didn't speak, just lifted his hand, still gripping hers, and held it against her cheek.

He said under his breath, "Oh God, Hilary!"

Ickfield High Street was deserted. It was twelve hours now since they'd met there in the sunshine – the longest time they had spent together. He circled the green and stopped just short of Conningley gateposts. As he switched off the ignition the soft background music faded away and there was total silence. They turned to each other at the same moment, and any last reservation she might have had vanished as his mouth found hers.

Mrs Hare saw the lights of the parked car as she came down the slope of the hill, the limp drained body of the last wood pigeon dangling from her hand. Miss Hilary no doubt, with that young Mr Sandys. Well, she'd be needing all the support he could give her tomorrow. It would be a difficult day for all of them, but praise be this had been her final journey up to the Stone. She'd become really nervous of it during this last week, dreading the proximity necessary to tip the blood into the little hollowed basin so greedily awaiting it. It would not have been without precedent for the Stone to have turned against her and slaked its thirst from her own body. Such an occurrence had taken place once, in the distant past, within hours of the arranged sacrifice.

She reached the little wooden gate in the cottage wall and slipped into the shadowed garden. A light in the back bedroom showed that Ben was still awake – reading his comics, no doubt. A great lump of a boy like that, turned fifteen now, and still reading comics. Still, it was no concern of hers. She wondered fleetingly if he'd miss her when she'd gone, but she'd been more like a housekeeper than a mother to him. And Sam, with his drooping moustache and watery bloodshot eyes: though they had lived technically as man and wife for two years, their lives had seldom touched. A base was all she had needed, within reach of the Stone and the one elected to serve it. In return she had cooked and cleaned and to give Sam his due he'd accepted the limitations of the arrangement with good grace. That Mrs White along the road would be glad enough to take over her duties when she'd gone, with no doubt a few added perks beside.

Gerda Hare smiled grimly as she tipped the pathetic little corpse she carried into the dust-bin and opened the back door.

Hilary stirred reluctantly. "I really must go."

"How early can I decently arrive tomorrow?"

"For breakfast if you like, as I did today!"

"I think that might be stretching it a bit! Ten o'clock?"

"I'll be waiting."

His arm tightened round her. "I don't want you to go."

Gently she extricated herself. "Thank you for a wonderful day, and for my lovely ring."

"I hope it will be the first of hundreds."

She laughed. "Days or rings?"

"Both. Hilary, I love you. I've never said that to anyone before."

"And I love you." She kissed him quickly and slipped out

of the car before he could pull her back. "Don't bother coming to the door with me, or I'll never get inside!"

"You have a point there. Good-night, my love. Sleep well."

She was gone. He drove slowly to the gate and watched her go up the drive and through the front door. A wonderful day, she had said: without doubt the most wonderful of his life, beyond all his wildest expectations. All the same, he found himself hoping he had not played too large a part in the actual breaking of her engagement, preferring to believe that the decision had been virtually reached before they'd met. Fleetingly he thought of the unknown Chris, somewhere in Africa. Sorry, mate, he thought. Hope you find someone else soon. Then on a surge of exaltation he started the car and turned in the direction of home.

Sixteen

Gavin said, "Did you ask Mrs Hare to come in today?"

Julia pulled the counterpane up the bed and smoothed it over the pillows. "Of course not. She never does, on Sundays."

"Well, she's here now, as large as life."

Julia straightened and stared across at him, fighting down a ridiculous sense of foreboding. "But what on earth for?"

"Search me. You'd better ask her."

She sighed, rubbing a hand over her forehead. "I suppose I shall have to, though I don't feel up to arguing the point. I didn't sleep well, and now Hilary says Adam Sandys will be here for lunch."

"In which case," Gavin said practically, "you could

probably do with a bit of extra help. Perhaps you transmitted a subconscious S.O.S. and the old girl picked it up!''

But instead of smiling Julia repressed a shudder and he put an arm round her. "Cheer up, darling, it isn't the end of the world! The weather's probably getting you down. We could do with a good storm to clear the air.''

When Julia reached the kitchen, Mrs Hare's appearance did nothing to dispel her misgivings. Her face was flushed, her mouth twitching and there was a feverish light in her eyes. Before Julia could speak, she said rapidly. "There was one or two things I didn't get through yesterday, mum, so I thought I'd pop up and finish them off.''

"Surely there was nothing that couldn't have waited till tomorrow?'' Julia tried to fight down her exasperation. The woman seemed unable to keep away. From the first, she'd insisted that one free day a week was sufficient and having reluctantly admitted to herself that she was less than comfortable in the presence of her 'daily', Julia found herself looking forward to having the house to themselves on Sundays.

The woman's eyes suddenly shifted away from her. Julia turned to see Vanessa standing in the doorway and immediately her irritation was swamped by anxiety. The girl looked pale and drawn and the expression in her eyes, Julia thought, with something approaching horror, was almost identical to that of Mrs Hare.

"Darling, what is it?'' she said sharply. "Are you ill?''

Vanessa dragged her eyes from the motionless woman to her mother's face. "I've rather a headache, that's all.''

"I believe you've got company for lunch?'' Mrs Hare said after a moment. "Since I'm here, I might as well stay and give you a hand.''

"There's really no need.'' Julia spoke more sharply than she'd intended. "It's a cold meal and everything's prepared.''

"I can at least lay the table and wash up afterwards.''

Her resistance crumbled. It was churlish to keep refusing the woman's offer of help, and as she'd told Gavin she was feeling less than her best today.

"All right," she said, and added stiffly, "Thank you."

Vanessa had wandered past her into the kitchen and was standing staring out of the window. Julia hesitated for a moment, then, unable to think of any excuse to take the girl out with her, turned and left the room.

Mrs Hare's tongue darted over her lips. "You know why I'm here. The appointed time has come."

A shiver rippled over the girl's thin body and without turning from the window she slowly nodded her head.

The oppressive, sunless heat was distressing to Marion. She lay on her bed with only a sheet over her wasted body and watched Brian pacing ceaselessly round the room. During the last couple of days his condition had deteriorated rapidly, and he'd become almost demented when she had innocently enquired how Vanessa had enjoyed the cream tea. If he'd only leave the room she could try to phone Julia and ask for help, but he had spent the entire morning circling it, stopping abruptly every now and again with his head slightly on one side as though he were listening for something. Once, hoping to distract and calm him, she had asked him to read to her but he hadn't seemed to hear.

Six strides to the window, the briefest of pauses, then a swing round and six paces back to the door. Marion wondered how much longer she could bear it without screaming at him to stop.

"Those two seem very thick," Gavin commented, nodding along the terrace to where Hilary and Adam were talking quietly together.

"Yes." With an effort Julia brought her thoughts from Vanessa to her elder daughter. "Did you notice the ring she's wearing? Apparently he bought it for her at the auction yesterday."

Gavin turned sharply. "A ring? He hasn't wasted much time, has he?"

"It's not an engagement ring – or at least, not officially. She's wearing it on her right hand."

"This is the first time I've met the fellow, of course, but you like him, don't you?"

"Very much, and his parents too. I think she could do a lot worse."

"Let's hope she knows her own mind this time."

"I don't think there's much doubt of that."

Nick came through the french windows and flopped on to the garden seat beside his parents. "Whew, it's hot, isn't it? Not a breath of air. The winch will be working flat out today. I think I'll wander up there for a while later. What time's lunch, Mum?"

"Any minute now. I'll ask Mrs Hare to take it in."

In the heavy light the dining-room took on a luminous green glow, reminding Julia of Gavin's comment about eating in a forest. The cold meal added to the fancy and she had the absurd impression that they were celebrating some pagan feast in a woodland glade, rather than sitting conventionally round her own dining-table. Certainly Mrs Hare, moving silently between them, placed each dish on the table as though taking part in a sacred rite.

Julia shook herself impatiently. It was, she told herself, simply the woman's unaccustomed presence at Sunday lunch which seemed to lend it an almost ominous importance. Nevertheless, she was relieved when the meal was over.

"Coffee on the terrace, everyone!" she said with forced gaiety.

"Not for me, thanks." Vanessa pushed her chair under the table. "I think I'll go up to my room for a while and try to shake off this headache."

"I won't bother with coffee either," Nick put in. "I'm going up to the club for a while. See you later."

Mrs Hare arrived on the terrace with the correct number

of coffee cups, despite the fact that no-one appeared to have told her of Nick and Vanessa's absence. Adam registered this fact and looked at the woman curiously. 'We seem to be plagued with hares!' he'd laughingly said to Hilary at one stage. Now, studying the woman's face, he was aware of a ripple of unease. There was a hidden excitement about her which disturbed him, though he could not have said why. Mistress Hare, the keeper of the spell-stones in the days of Clarissa Henry, and now this woman involved with the family at Conningley a significant hundred years on. Looking at her closed, secretive face it was almost possible to convince himself they were one and the same.

Shaking himself free of his fancies, he took the cup and saucer Hilary was holding out to him

Vanessa lay on her bed, the tolmaen round her neck. There were whispers and voices all round her, advising, cajoling, instructing. She could feel beads of perspiration along her hairline.

"No!" she protested involuntarily. "Don't make me – please! I can't do it!" And the voices soothed and stroked her quivering mind, encouraging, gently insisting.

Bran! Her memory flooded with a picture of him. Bran the Blessen Raven, with his black hair and silky beard, his fine dark eyes. A noble sacrifice indeed, the Wondrous Head of Bran! Could it be this the Stone had craved throughout all these years! Might this then be the final atonement, the end of the cycle?

Her fingers moved convulsively over the stones, rubbing, rubbing, as her mind reached out across the torrid airless day, down the hillsides and over the valley to Kimble, where Brian Cresswell eagerly awaited its summons.

At last! She had sent for him! Exultation filled him, seeming to push out from inside his head until he felt it must surely burst. He put both hands to his temples and the touch of his own fingers reminded him of hers, of that odd ritual caress she had given him. And now she was waiting up by the Stone!

He glanced down at Marion, but she had fallen into a restless sleep. For a few seconds he stared down at her dispassionately. Then, excitement rising in him, he went swiftly down the stairs, and met Miss Fergusson in the dark hallway.

"I'm going out," he told her. "Tell my wife I don't know when I'll be back." Or, indeed, if! he thought, more on a wave of hope than premonition, as he hurried to the waiting car.

The thought waves in Vanessa's brain pulsed and swelled, pulsed and swelled. '*We serve the Stone*'. Scenes were flickering in front of her closed eyes: her own body, unconscious on the threshold of Conningley, with Mrs Hare standing over her; the dark shape of the elemental at the well; the Stone on the hillside, and finally Bran's Head, wondrous and shining with immortality.

Uncle Bran, No – Bran the Blessed, son of Llyr. She gave a little groan, twisting her head from side to side in a last futile attempt to dissociate herself. Then, unwillingly, her eyes opened and once more, as in the memory just gone, the figure of Mrs Hare loomed above her.

"Come!" she said, her voice vibrating with excitement. "It is time."

Vanessa obediently sat up and swung her feet to the floor. Her fingers, independent of her volition, were flexing and stretching, caressing the empty air as though craving the hard, satisfying feel of Brian's skull beneath them, the thick hair, the line of his jaw, the cords in his strong neck. She gave a choked little sound and Mrs Hare said quickly, "Peace, my lovely. All is arranged."

The girl dragged her eyes up to the fanatical face above her. "But – how?"

"The means will be provided. Trust in the power of the Stone. No axe this time, to allow talk of premeditation. It will be made clear to you when the victim appears – and he is approaching even now. We must hurry."

Passively Vanessa allowed herself to be led quietly through the front door of her home, down the drive and round the crescent to the main road. Her family's presence on the terrace shut off the usual route to the hillside.

Mrs Hare's trembling hands opened the front gate of her own cottage and she guided the girl round the side of the house, across the tiny garden to the gate giving on to the lower slope of the hill. In a dream Vanessa walked beside her, confused images playing across the dulled mirror of her mind. How long since she had come this way? Eighty, a hundred years? And the great machines that circled soundlessly overhead – what part had they in this ancient ritual?

They emerged from the trees alongside the top of Conningley garden. Behind the wall the well would be crouching, impassive yet having played its small part in the recurring drama.

"Now, my sweeting, my brave and lovely one, I can come no further. My work is done. From this point you go alone. You know what you must do."

A flicker crossed the girl's face. She started to shake her head, but fumblingly, fearfully her hand crept up to the weight of the tolmaen lying implacably against her breast. Satisfied, Mrs Hare gave a quick nod and, powerless against the pressures of centuries, Vanessa turned and obediently began to stumble up the hill.

Julia came hurrying out on to the terrace. "Adam, would you excuse us if we leave you for a while?" She turned to Hilary. "Marion's just been on the phone. She seems upset about something and wants Daddy and me to go straight over. We should be back well before you have to leave for the hospital."

"I hope it's nothing serious. Give her my love."

"Explain to Vanessa when she wakes, will you?" Distractedly Julia hurried inside again and minutes later they heard the car start up.

"Mother's somewhat flustered today," Hilary remarked. "I think she's worried about Van. I noticed quite a change in her myself when I came home yesterday. She seems withdrawn somehow, and she hardly touched her lunch, did you notice? Believe me, that alone is unusual enough to give rise to concern."

"She did strike me as being rather on edge. So, come to that, did Mistress Hare."

Hilary turned to look at him. "And that's odd, too. No-one knows what she's doing here today. Sunday's supposed to be her day off, and Mother didn't ask her to come in."

Adam said slowly, "You know, I don't like it. Any of it. I have a feeling things are rushing towards a climax."

"The Stone, you mean?" Hilary gazed at him wide-eyed.

"It would provide a strong reason, wouldn't you say, for Mrs Hare being on hand, even on her free day? And Vanessa, as we've discovered, is susceptible to atmosphere." He paused, thinking of the spell-stones which his promise to her had still barred him from mentioning to Hilary. If indeed the Stone was moving towards fulfilment, the spell-stones must be supercharged with energy and that could hardly fail to have an effect on the girl in whose possession they were. He should have insisted that she handed them over before this, he thought worriedly. After all, look at the effect they'd had on Clarissa Henry.

He stood up abruptly and Hilary glanced at him in surprise.

"Come on, let's go up and have a look at it. I want to see for myself how – stable it is."

"But what about Vanessa? She'll wonder where everyone's gone – and we can't leave her alone with Mrs Hare."

"I should think," Adam said grimly, "that Mrs Hare left some time ago. Would you like to go and check?"

Hilary ran into the house, emerging a minute or two later. "Yes, you're right. The lunch things have all been put away and her hat and bag have gone."

"Right. Then all we need do is leave a note for Vanessa telling her we'll be back soon."

"You really think something's going to happen?"

"I don't know, but we can't just sit here wondering. Hurry!"

Minutes later, with the note duly left for Vanessa, they set off up the garden and on to the hill. They didn't notice the figure of Mrs Hare dart quickly back behind a tree as they emerged from the gate. She stared after them gloatingly. Don't think you can stop it, my ducks! All will take place as decreed and before darkness falls tonight the Stone will have received its dues.

Nick saw Adam and Hilary as they came over the brow of the hill and hurried towards them, relief spreading over his face.

"Thank goodness you're here. Look, I'm worried about old Brian. I found his car parked down by the club house – you know how he's always denied coming up here? This time I was determined to catch him out so I started to look for him. I did catch sight of him at one point, but he managed to give me the slip. Hil, he was behaving awfully oddly. He seemed – ill, somehow."

"Maybe that's why Marion phoned the parents."

"Brian's up here?" Adam cut in sharply. "Vanessa's 'Bran'?"

They both stared at him, their hearts beginning to thud at the urgency in his voice

'What is it, Adam?" Hilary was suddenly frightened. The Head of Bran, she thought confusedly. "You can't possibly think –"

"What I think," Adam said grimly, "is that we'd better find him, and as soon as possible."

Nick said plaintively, "Will someone please explain? What are you two on about?"

"Where was he when you saw him, Nick?"

"Dodging around between the gliders."

The noise of the winch started up close behind them, making them jump, and they turned to watch the distant approach of the glider and the rushing in of the murderous steel cable, taut and almost invisible like some deadly spider's thread. Slowly the machine lifted, the angle of the cable increased sharply and, as the glider gained height, the cable was released and fell back to the ground.

"Now the truck will take it back to the launch point for the next plane," Nick explained, his obsession with the sport momentarily replacing his concern over Brian.

"And Brian's interested in all this?" Hilary demanded.

"I suppose he must be. At any rate I've seen him up here several times, over by the Stone."

Adam turned sharply, his eyes scanning the megalith from a distance of some two hundred yards. "No-one seems to be near it at the moment. Actually, that was what we came to look at but we'd better concentrate on finding Brian first."

On the far side of the Stone, hidden alike from the winch and the ascent from Conningley, Vanessa stood spread-eagled, eyes closed. She sensed that he was not far away. *Come to me*, she willed him. *You have sworn your fealty; now you must put it to the supreme test.* In a frenzy of concentration she stiffened, arching her back, and the sudden straining movement loosed the last worn knot in the thong about her neck. As it came apart the tolmaen slid down her body and dropped into the grass at the base of the Stone.

Vanessa's eyes shuttered open and she looked about her in bewilderment. Her last clear memory was of lying on her bed at home. At her back the Stone felt rough and some current within it prickled at her skin through the thin shirt. With a shrug of distaste she pushed herself away from it, and her foot knocked against the fallen tolmaen. Hesitantly she stooped to pick it up and slipped it for the last time into the pocket of her jeans. Then, unaccountably anxious to be away from the Stone and all its emanations, she hurried home.

There was no-one on the terrace but a note on the table informed her that her parents had gone to Kimble and Adam and Hilary for a walk. The pain in her head which had been troubling her all day returned with sudden intensity. Stumblingly she made her way back up the stairs and had only time to fall across the bed before complete darkness overcame her.

Brain wiped the sweat from his eyes with an impatient hand. *I'm coming, beloved, I'm coming*! If only that blasted boy hadn't spotted him, making it necessary to waste several precious minutes in diversionary tactics! But he could hardly approach the Goddess of the Stone with Nick trotting determinedly at his heels! A travesty of a smile twisted Brian's mouth. Was farce always so close to tragedy?

He frowned, confused by the word his mind had unhesitatingly supplied. What tragedy could there be in his willing subjugation to the dictates of the past? He would gladly sacrifice all that he had for the chance to be with her, however briefly. *My love, my wise and wonderful mistress – I'm coming*.

Urgency overcoming caution, he broke cover and began to run up the grassy slope towards the outline of the Stone. In front of him and to his left, the winch crouched, a modern aberration in this timeless setting, and the great lumbering glider, as clumsy on the ground as some prehistoric bird, rocked across the ground away to his right. No matter – she was waiting! He could feel her reaching out for him, encouraging, beckoning –

He stumbled to a halt, looking about him in bewilderment. From one second to the next the signals had ceased, leaving him lost, without guidance. Could she have tired of waiting for him? Damn Nick and his importunities! *Wait – oh my love I'm almost there! Wait for me!*

In an excess of anguish he hurled himself forward, oblivious of Nick's sudden cry of alarm over to the left, blind to the unseen barrier of the cable, razor sharp, soaring shoulder high as the glider left the ground. The last sight to meet his straining eyes was the ruthless, implacable Stone.

On the hill path above Conningley, Gerda Hare stood motionless, tense and waiting. She had seen Vanessa's unexpected return and was at a loss how to understand it. Pray Taranis nothing had gone wrong at this stage. She hesitated, agonizingly unsure whether to seek out Vanessa for an explanation, or venture up the hill to see what was taking place. Above her in the colourless sky two gliders circled and swooped. And as she stood undecided, over the still afternoon came the sound she had been waiting for, a thin, high keening.

It was done! The Screeching Stone had accepted its tribute.

For a second longer she stood there, hands clasped and face transfigured. Then she turned and hurried away down the hill.

"Oh God, oh God, oh God, oh God!" Hilary knew somehow that the voice was hers, muffled in Adam's chest as she pressed her face against him. His arm, tightly about her, was shaking, and somewhere near at hand she could hear Nick's agonized retching. But transcending all these immediate sensations was the ghastly picture emblazoned on her retina, of the jerking, twitching body under the wire and the obscenely rolling ball that was the head of Brian.

Now voices, running footsteps, exclamations of incredulous horror were all about them and she heard Adam's voice, strained and shaken: "Yes. Yes, we saw it happen." At last she lifted her head to support him in what must now be faced.

The winch driver, grey-faced, was saying repeatedly, "I

never saw him! So help me, I never saw him! I was
concentrating on the glider, I didn't notice anything else.
And God love us, who'd expect anyone to approach in front
of the winch? It's the first, basic safety rule!"

"No-one's blaming you, Bill," someone said with shaky
sympathy. "Look, we'll have to move the poor devil. We
can't leave him lying here in – in separate pieces. I presume
someone's gone to phone for an ambulance? Help me to lay
him out decently, Bill, until they get here. That stone slab
over there will do admirably."

Hilary started forward involuntarily. "No, not there!"
she began, but Adam caught her arm.

"Don't stop them, darling. For God's sake let the Stone
receive its head. We don't want to go through all this
again."

It must have seemed a ready-made mortuary slab, that
low altar where Vanessa had once lain. And upon it the
willing sacrifice was reverently laid, an anonymous jacket
decorously covering the repellent severance of head and
body.

Hilary said suddenly, "We must go back to Vanessa.
Suppose she should wake and come up here looking for us.
Nick –" she reached out blindly for her brother's hand. "All
right?"

He nodded whitely, averting his eyes from the covered
shape on the Stone.

"If the police need us for a statement," Adam said
tersely to the nearest man, "we'll all be down at
Conningley."

In her bedroom Vanessa awoke, stretching luxuriously. All
trace of her headache had disappeared and with it the
strains, stresses and uncertainties which seemed to have
bedevilled her ever since she came to Conningley. All at
once she felt gloriously alive and free. As she sat up the
spell-stones in her pocket dug into her and she drew them
out, looking at them in faint bewilderment. They felt cold

and unusually heavy in her hand, and the thong on the tolmaen had come untied. She tried to think why they had seemed so important – something to do with O-level results? The memory eluded her. In any case, she had no further use for them. Adam could have them, since he seemed to want them so much. In the meantime she felt ravenously hungry, and wondered hopefully if tea was ready.

Adam said, "Are you sure you're all right, darling? You wouldn't like me to phone the hospital and explain?"

"No, I – I think I need to get away for a while." She looked up at him. "Adam, am I completely mad, or was what happened exactly what we've been waiting for?"

"I don't know, darling. I honestly don't know."

"Up there, you said –"

"I know. I'm sorry. Put it down to the heat of the moment."

"But the fact remains that the severed head was actually laid out on the Stone, exactly according to the book. Could it really have been coincidence?"

"God knows. Even if it wasn't, at least we can be thankful that this time no-one was called on to engineer it personally. Outwardly at least it was simply a terrible accident."

"That's how the parents see it, of course. They needn't ever know the full implications, need they?"

"I don't see why. Nick may well put two and two together when the shock wears off, but I'm sure he'll agree it's best to keep our suspicions to ourselves. Nothing could ever be proved, anyway."

She looked up suddenly. "What about Van, though? She knows the legend. Surely she can't help but see the connection?"

"That's what I was afraid of, but she didn't seem to, did she? Her reaction was just perfectly normal shock and grief. You know, considering how intrigued she was by the diary

when she first found it, it's strange that she should have lost interest in it so completely: almost as though some advance safety mechanism clicked into position to cushion her against what was going to happen."

"You were part of that safety mechanism, in not handing it back to her. Just think what might have happened if by some ghastly chain of events she'd felt compelled to bring it all about herself, as poor Clarissa did."

"Subconsciously that's been worrying me all along, especially when she wouldn't part with those spell-stones, but as you saw she handed them over just now without so much as a tremor. We can only be thankful that despite all the odds, she at least was completely uninvolved."

When by Tuesday morning Mrs Hare had still not put in an appearance, Julia forced herself to go in search of her. Throughout the previous day, though surprised by her non-appearance, her mind had been too full of Brian and Marion to bother about such household matters. Presumably the woman was ill – she hadn't seemed herself on Sunday – though so exemplary had her previous behaviour been that Julia would have expected some notification of the fact.

However, when she walked up the cottage path and rang the bell, it was to be greeted with unexpected and bewildering news. Mr Hare opened the door, lugubrious and watery-eyed.

"She's gawn, mum," he told her, ushering her into the spotless kitchen. "Just clean gawn, as suddenly as she come two year since."

"Two years?" Julia echoed. "But I thought –" Her eyes went to the gawky youth at the sink, sullenly peeling potatoes.

"Ben's by me first wife, mum. Edith, Gawd rest her soul. Passed on these three years back. We was finding it hard to manage, Ben and me, and it seemed a blessing when Gerda arrived on the doorstep. Said she'd heard I was alone and

was prepared to cook and keep house, provided I married her for decency's sake. And it turned out well, considering. She was a good worker and we never went hungry."

"But – surely she'll be back?" Julia couldn't understand his acceptance of the extraordinary situation.

Mr Hare shook his head gloomily. "No, we'll not set eyes on her again, take my word for it."

"You won't even try to trace her?"

"Wouldn't know where to start, would I? Wasn't one for talking of her private affairs, wasn't Gerda. All I know is that her name was Hare before we wed. Funny, that. Perhaps that's why she chose us."

Defeated, Julia could only murmur her condolences and make her way home again.

So it was over, and after a week or two of shocked excitement, the village settled back to its habitual peace. From time to time Vanessa still wept over Brian's death, but he had really been lost to her since that inexplicable confrontation in the lane, and it was then that her most bitter tears had been shed.

On the hill above Ickfield all was calm again. The Druid Stone, satiated at last, sank back into its petrified coma and several nights of heavy rain obliterated all traces of the blood which had so recently been spilled there. There was nothing to alarm the pheasant which alighted on it to preen its feathers, and a small rabbit, scuttling from the hovering menace of a hawk, hid in safety under its benign shadow.